Everyone noticed us approaching and grew silent. The crowd parted to reveal Prince Roquefort and his ogres leaning against an elaborately decorated wagon. One from the king's personal collection, obviously. Sitting atop the wagon was a large cage, containing four irritated-looking Swampfrogs.

"So you didn't wuss out after all," the prince said in a voice like nails on a chalkboard. His eyes were at half-mast, giving him a look both sinister and dim-witted.

"No, no. I'm all in, Your Splendiferousness," I said as I bowed sarcastically, hearing a little nervous squeak out of Kevin. I was acting pretty tough, but I'll admit I was nervous. I even had that nervous have-to-pee feeling. Why does your body always want you to go to the bathroom when you get nervous? Maybe it figures there's not too much trouble you can get into in the john.

OTHER BOOKS YOU MAY ENJOY

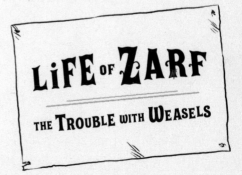

PUFFIN BOOKS
An imprint of Penguin Random House LLC
375 Hudson Street
New York, New York 10014

First published in the United States of America by Dial Books,
an imprint of Penguin Group (USA) LLC, 2014
Published by Puffin Books, an imprint of Penguin Random House LLC, 2016

THE LIBRARY OF CONGRESS HAS CATALOGED THE DIAL BOOKS EDITION AS FOLLOWS:
Harrell, Rob.
Life of Zarf: the trouble with weasels / Rob Harrell.
pages cm.
Summary: As a troll, Zarf Belford is at the bottom of the social ladder at Cotswin Middle School, but when the king goes missing and his insufferable son takes control, Zarf leads his friends Kevin and Chester on a rescue mission.
ISBN 978-0-8037-4103-4 (hardcover)
[1. Adventure and adventurers—Fiction. 2. Trolls—Fiction. 3. Characters in literature—Fiction. 4. Princes—Fiction. 5. Imaginary creatures—Fiction. 6. Middle schools—Fiction. 7. Schools—Fiction. 8. Humorous stories.]
I. Title. II. Title: Trouble with Weasels.
PZ7.H2348Lif 2014
[Fic]—dc23
2014002795

Puffin Books ISBN 978-0-14-751171-3

Printed in the United States of America

1 3 5 7 9 10 8 6 4 2

For Mom and Dad

INTRODUCTIONS ARE IN ORDER

Zarf.

That's the name they gave me.

Not a majestic name, by any means. You don't hear about many kings or leaders named "Zarf the All-Powerful" or "Zarf the Merciless." Not a melodic name, either. Sort of falls out of your mouth in one big lump and just lays there.

It's also a really easy name to mock, seeing as how it rhymes with "barf." But I'm doing with it what I can. It's a family name, after all.

I am a troll. I know the term "troll" has become a popular insult these days, but I mean it literally. I come from a long line of Eastern Prairie Trolls. My grandfather (also named Zarf) is the one you've probably heard the most about, what with the "billy goats gruff" business. That story got a lot of traction in the papers and the anti-troll literature. He's still living that whole thing down.

And before you ask, yes, my family does live under a bridge. My folks claim they rent the place because it's in a good school district and the price is right, but I'm not a complete idiot—my dad and Gramps still get their kicks scaring the stuffing out of unsuspecting bridge-goers from time to time.

KINGDOM
COME

We live in the village of Cotswin in the kingdom of Notswin, and I can assure you that nothing exciting has happened around here since Goldie Locks was in short pants. And that was a LOOONG time ago. Old Lady Locks has been the lunch lady at my school since time began, slopping out porridge to generation after generation of Cotswinians. And her hair is a lot more blue than it is gold these days. Anyways, Cotswin is a fairly quiet place where kids my age are free to perish from acute boredom, and often do.

LOOKS LIKE IT WAS THAT SOCIAL STUDIES LECTURE THAT DID HIM IN.

Sure, there's your occasional small dragon attack or croquet match, but mostly the days just drag out like the last few minutes of algebra class. That is, until the last couple of weeks, I should say.

I attend Cotswin Middle School for the Criminally Insane. Okay, I added that last part, but it's not far from the truth. Good old Cotswin—Home of the Prancing Knights. (Trust me, no one is happy about that mascot name. Petitions have been filed.)

School is tough. In a lot of ways. Trolls aren't exactly known for their book smarts. I'm doing my best to overcome my heritage, but it ain't easy. I was doing a word problem the other day in class and actually caught myself grunting. Grunting! So embarrassing. Fortunately it was kind of a quiet grunt. More like a gruntlet.

This is one of the reasons it's important to surround yourself with a quality crew . . .

SIX DEGREES OF KEVIN

KEVIN

Two weeks ago on a rainy Tuesday morning, my friend Kevin stopped by my house like he does every day on the way to school. His full name is Kevin Littlepig, of the world-famous Littlepigs. You've probably heard of them. His family lives a few streets over in an epic mansion called Littlepig Manor.

BRICK, FOR OBVIOUS REASONS

After their well-known encounters with a certain huffing and puffing wolf, Kevin's dad and his uncles got into the construction business and made a small fortune. They're constantly pushing Kevin to become a structural engineer. Given their family history, I guess I can't blame them.

Kevin and I have been best friends since second grade, when I traded him a leg of my mom's mutton for an extra milk at lunch. My mom makes the best mutton this side of Notswin Castle. Ask anyone. Kevin couldn't stop going on about that mutton. He still talks about it—like a broken record. This particular day I'm gonna tell you about, he arrived looking pretty shaken up, but I still noticed him sniffing around the kitchen just in case. Seriously, he's like an un-dead mutton zombie or something.

SAVORY...
SUCCULENT...
DELICIOUS...
MUTTON!

Kevin has issues. Lots of 'em. For starters, there's his height. His last name, Littlepig, really couldn't be more appropriate. He stands about knee-high to a hill ferret, and boy is he ever sensitive about it. I once saw him burst into tears when he ordered pancakes and the waitress asked if he wanted a "short stack."

He also might be the most nervous individual in the world. It can be kind of annoying, the way he's always worrying and wringing his hooves. If there were a Stress Olympics, he'd take the gold all day long—but then he'd probably drop dead from a panic attack on the winners' podium.

I swear to you, the other day on the way to school he admitted to me that he'd been worrying

WHOOO.
FEELIN' A LITTE
LIGHT-HEADED
OVER HERE.

that he wasn't worrying enough. That makes my head hurt to even think about. He's kind of a freak-show that way.

So Kevin showed up at my place and as we were walking through a steady drizzle to school, I could tell something was bothering him. When he's really worked up, he lets out these little whimpers and twitches a lot.

"What's up with you? You're like a fart in a skillet."

He looked up with wide eyes. "I don't know what that means. Is that bad? That's bad, isn't it?"

"No, it just means you're hopping around a lot. What's on your mind?"

So as we cut across the Enchanted Field, Kevin nervously filled me in on the latest village news. A group of woodsmen from Wallen, the next village over from ours, had been attacked by a herd of Snuffweasels. Details were foggy about the woodsmen's injuries, but the town was understandably flipping out. There hadn't been a Snuffweasel sighting in ten years or more, and everyone was pretty happy about that. If you aren't familiar with them, Snuffweasels are nothing to sneeze at. They stand about seven feet tall with mouths full of teeth like broken glass. They're sort of like Swampweasels, but quite a bit snuffier.

7 FT. 1 IN.

5 FT. 10 IN.

AVERAGE
WOODSMAN

AVERAGE
SNUFFWEASEL

"I heard they ate one guy's face and toes." Kevin shuddered.

"This is fantastic," I said in a hushed tone.

"WHAT?? How can you say that??"

"No!" I quickly backpedaled. "Not that people were hurt! That's horrible. Just the fact that there are Snufffweasels out there. I thought they were pretty much extinct."

"Well, that's easy for you to say! You're not made of delicious bacon! I hear they have a real taste for pork products!"

Kevin was really worked up now, so I just patted him on the back and kept my thoughts to myself as we arrived at school.

· 4 ·

WELCOME TO
THE JUNGLE

Cotswin Middle School is a damp old dungeon of a building, and on rainy days like today it reeks of dark mold and soggy Tater Tots. It probably bothers me more than most, as trolls can smell a mincemeat pie from three villages away. No joke.

SNIFF

I'M GETTING BOYSENBERRY... A GRAHAM CRACKER CRUST... AND IT'S BEEN OUT OF THE OVEN THIRTY MINUTES OR SO.

The entryway was full of kids stamping around and shaking off the rain. I was bent over drying off my soggy feet when one of the football giants casually pushed my backpack up over my head, pitching me forward onto my nose with my shirt shoved up around my ears.

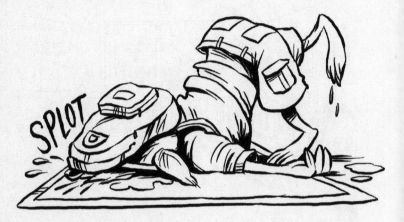

Of course, everyone got a huge kick out of me with a face full of muddy mat water, and laughter rang out in the wet foyer. Savages! Neanderthals! Anyway . . . Welcome to Cotswin.

Let me say a word about the social ladder at Cotswin. I've taken the time to draw up a visual aid for you.

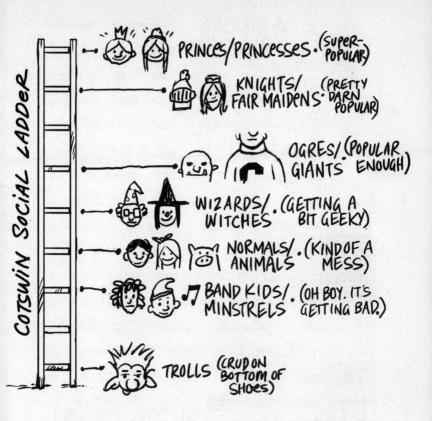

COTSWIN SOCIAL LADDER

PRINCES/PRINCESSES. (SUPER-POPULAR)

KNIGHTS/FAIR MAIDENS. (PRETTY DARN POPULAR)

OGRES/GIANTS. (POPULAR ENOUGH)

WIZARDS/WITCHES. (GETTING A BIT GEEKY)

NORMALS/ANIMALS. (KIND OF A MESS)

BAND KIDS/MINSTRELS. (OH BOY. IT'S GETTING BAD.)

TROLLS (CRUD ON BOTTOM OF SHOES)

At the top, you've got your princes and princesses. They're the true "populars." Then come your knights and fair maidens. Just below that are the jocks, made up mostly of giants and ogres. Then come your wizards. They're kind of all science-y and geeky, but they can also do some pretty cool tricks.

Then comes the general population— just your average kids: elves, gnomes, enchanted animals, etc. Below them are the minstrels, or band kids. A few kids are in rock minstrel bands, which elevates their status, but for the most part, this is where they settle in the social pecking order. Then, finally, on the bottom rung you have your trolls. The princesses and maidens aren't exactly lining up to go to the school dances with my size-22, two hairy left feet. I try not to take it personally.

Trolls have had it crappy since time began. It's just the way it's always been.

When I arrived at my locker, Kevin's and my other good friend Chester was waiting for me with a big goofy grin.

A few words about Chester. First, I would say that he's my Second Best Friend. Technically, he's right up there with Kevin, but I've known Kevin a couple years longer, so . . . you know. He gets the Number 2 slot and seems okay with that. But if they were in some sort of weird best friend race, it'd be a photo finish.

KEVIN
(BY A NOSE)

Chester Flintwater is the son of the Notswin Court Jester. If you're not familiar with what a jester does, they're sort of like a clown whose job is to make the king laugh. They tell jokes, smash bottles over their head, fall down, shove breadsticks up their nose—whatever it takes to get a smile out of the big guy.

It is assumed that when Chester's dad retires, Chester will take over the position of jester. And yes, this will make him "Chester the Jester." This is the kind of rib-splitting hilarity one can expect when they have a clown for a father.

There is one problem, however. My friend Chester, God love him, is the least funny person I know. He tries. Oh, man does he try, but it's just not in him. He's constantly studying joke books, listening to old tapes of the *Classic Days of Ye Olde Comedy* show, and practicing his pratfalls. He actually keeps a rubber chicken on him at all times, no matter how many times I tell him they aren't funny.

I think he lives in a bit of a state of panic, knowing what's going to be expected of him. I'm telling you . . . it's painful to watch at times.

Chester saw me looking all disheveled and muddy, and tried to think up a witty quip.

"Wow. Look at you. You look like a . . . uh . . ."

I waited. It's best to let him try to work these things out.

"Like a . . . You look like . . ." His eyes searched the ground, trying to find something even remotely funny. You could almost hear the gears grinding in his head.

Finally his shoulders sagged. "Ah, I got nothin'. But I was close."

"You're getting there. Just keep practicing." I gave him an encouraging smile as I popped open my locker.

Suddenly he brightened and pulled a wadded piece of paper out of his back pocket. "Did you see this?" He unfolded it and showed me a public notice—one of the official ones from the castle. I took the sheet and read it quickly.

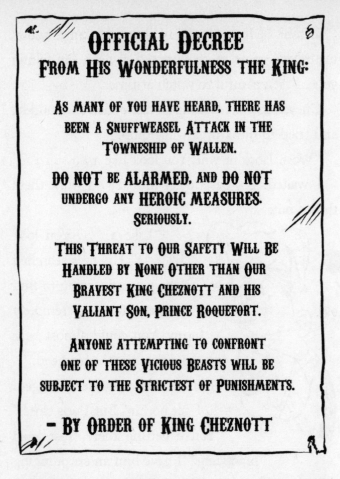

OFFICIAL DECREE
FROM HIS WONDERFULNESS THE KING:

AS MANY OF YOU HAVE HEARD, THERE HAS
BEEN A SNUFFWEASEL ATTACK IN THE
TOWNESHIP OF WALLEN.

DO NOT BE ALARMED, AND DO NOT
UNDERGO ANY HEROIC MEASURES.
SERIOUSLY.

THIS THREAT TO OUR SAFETY WILL BE
HANDLED BY NONE OTHER THAN OUR
BRAVEST KING CHEZNOTT AND HIS
VALIANT SON, PRINCE ROQUEFORT.

ANYONE ATTEMPTING TO CONFRONT
ONE OF THESE VICIOUS BEASTS WILL BE
SUBJECT TO THE STRICTEST OF PUNISHMENTS.

– BY ORDER OF KING CHEZNOTT

I looked up at Chester and we were able to hold it
together for about 1.3 seconds before we both burst
out laughing.

"His valiant son Prince Roquefort?" I snorted,
which brought even louder laughter from Chester. I
went on. "Lord help us if our savior is Young Prince

Cheeseball. Maybe the plan is to let a Snuffweasel chomp down on the little nimrod and then barf to death." I was on a roll. "The day I put my safety in the Good Prince's hands is the day I . . ." And that, friends, was when I noticed that Chester was no longer laughing. That was when I heard a clearing of a throat and that oh, so annoying voice pipe up from behind and a bit below me . . .

"Oh, I do hope you're having a good laugh, Troll."

· 5 ·

ROQUEFORT ON THE SIDE

It was, of course, Prince Roquefort. Flanked by two of his ogre bodyguards. Timing has never been my strong suit, but this was really bad.

Prince Roquefort is not a pleasant person. To be more accurate, I would rank him as one of the slimiest, sneakiest, most horrible people to ever slither through Cotswin Middle School. But I should let you judge his horribleness for yourself.

"Hmm. Maybe I should report you to my father."

This was a classic Roquefort threat, but I could tell he was really steaming this time. "Wait . . . who's my father? Oh, that's right. He's the KING. As in, the man who could crush your stupid little troll family like so many floppy-eared bugs. So maybe you should watch your stupid troll mouth."

I knew these were empty threats. King Cheznott was considered a kind and fair king. A beloved king. Every troll in the kingdom had a warm place in their heart for him, as he'd done more for troll rights than any king since King Cleo. His first

MORE CHEESE FOR EVERYONE!

act as a young king had been signing the Troll Act of '57, outlawing Punch-A-Troll Day for good.

My parents and Gramps could go on forever about him. How he had sired a human skid mark like Roquefort was anyone's guess. But it wouldn't do any good to get even further on the bad side of the king's son. Besides, those ogre guards were not so subtly baring their teeth at me. I was seething, but I clenched my jaw and fists and kept my mouth shut.

"Where's your other friend, the pig? Maybe the three of you together would have the courage to stand up to me rather than carry on about me when you think I'm not around." He had one of those gross stringy white spit things going between his lips when he spoke, and it somehow made me even angrier.

NASTY!

And then . . . Prince Roquefort, the tiny tyrant of Cotswin, took things one step too far. He stood up on his toes and got as close to my face as he could. He spoke slowly and in a soft tone so that the crowd that had gathered had to lean in to catch every word.

"You know what you and your friends are?" His hot breath smelled like one of your stinkier cheeses.

"You know what you are to this school? I'm going to tell you, because everyone else knows. You three are nothing but . . ."

STINK DRAGONS.

There was an audible gasp from the students gathered around. And then I saw red.

6

YOU'RE DRAGON ME DOWN

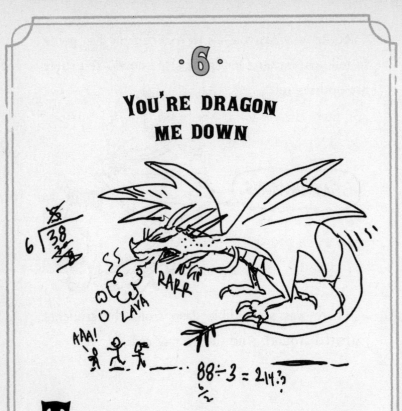

There are several types of dragons in our region. You've got your Night Dragons, your Swamp Dragons . . . Then you've got your really cool ones, like Lava Dragons. Lava Dragons are the ones everyone draws on their folders and has posters of in their bedrooms.

They're wicked-cool-looking, they shoot molten lava, and there are story after story about Lava Dragon battles in all of the coolest history books.

Then, you have your smaller, nuisance dragons. Your Plump Dragons, your Roof Dragons. These are more like big rats or birds than actual scary dragons. My dad has to put up plastic scaretrolls around our bridge to keep the Roof Dragons from pooping all over the house.

And then, unfortunately, there are Stink Dragons. A Stink Dragon is one of the foulest, smelliest creatures in all of the world.

One single Stink Dragon can bring down the property value of an entire village. They slither around leaving an awful sulfur-smelling trail of goo wherever they go. The village of Handel had an infestation of Stink Dragons two years ago and it just ruined them. They ended up burning the whole town down and starting over, just to get rid of that disgusting lingering fart smell. Nobody likes Stink Dragons. Period. End of story.

So, calling someone a Stink Dragon is such an offensive put-down, I have to admit I'd never heard it said before. When Prince Roquefort said that to me, it was as if all the air left the building. Suddenly, everything in my vision went red, the hairs stood up on my ears, and I did something I swore I would never do. I pushed Roquefort. Hard.

Now, Roquefort is not a big guy. He's actually shorter than Kevin, which is saying something.

Granted, he's round enough that I didn't think he'd go down as easy as he did. But down he went. Right on his stupid butt. His little prince hat went flying and Roquefort was laid out flat. I knew immediately I was in trouble.

One of the prince's brainless ogres jumped into action and grabbed me tightly by both arms while the other quickly checked Roquefort for injuries. As he was helped to his feet, the tiny tyrant's face was a dark red, verging on purple. I'm not sure if it was from anger or embarrassment, or maybe both. He was so mad, I thought his head might pop like a balloon (and kind of hoped it would). He spun on his ogre henchmen and yelled, "UP!! Up! Up!" The larger ogre, I think his name is Buddy or something, picked up the prince and held him right in my face.

"You just made a true enemy, rodent!" he sputtered, spit flying. (Technically, trolls are not part of the rodent family, but I decided to let that one slide.) "I challenge you to a JOUST!!" Let me tell you, the crowd was eating this up. They were murmuring up a storm.

Now, a middle school joust is different from the ones you see knights in armor doing in the movies. It involves riding on the backs of oversized Swampfrogs, and the lances used are made out of Nerf. Which isn't to say it isn't kind of dangerous. Swampfrogs hop at a pretty good clip, and a Nerf lance can knock you off your ride. So I didn't take this challenge lightly.

SWAMP-FROG

"You're on," I said through clenched teeth. I'm not sure what I was thinking. "When? After school?"

Roquefort put his hands on his hips and thought for a moment. "No. I have harpsichord lessons right after school. How about tomorrow before school?"

This gave me pause. "Seriously? Before school? I'm not exactly a morning person."

Roquefort pulled out his phone and began tapping away at it.

"Hmmm. What about later this evening? Like six-ish? Behind the gym?"

That worked for me. "I'll be there." We quickly exchanged contact info. As Roquefort and his thugs walked off, I felt the tension drain out of me, leaving me feeling like a big steaming pile of stupid.

TICK TICK

As the crowd dispersed and Chester and I set off for class, I overheard someone quietly snicker and say, "Stink Dragons. That's so perfect." It probably wouldn't have hurt so much if it didn't feel so true.

7

DINING IN
DISTRESS

I THINK I'M
GONNA THROW UP.

We were at lunch, and Kevin had just heard
the whole story. Word of my dust-up had
spread through the school quickly, but he hadn't
learned the gory details until just then.

"You always feel like you're going to throw up,"
I said as I peeked inside my lunchbox to see what
my mom had packed in there this morning.

"But this is bad. This is really bad. He's the
prince! He could throw us in prison or some-

thing. I'd get eaten alive in prison! Literally!"

"Calm yourself. And besides, it's just me he's all bent about." I patted Kevin on the back. Chester nodded vigorously and tried to talk through a mouth full of peanut butter and mulberry preserves.

"Ifsh 'onna be fine. You'll shee."

Kevin actually looked a little green around the gills. "Zarf is gonna die! I can't eat. There's no way I could eat anything." He pushed his lunch away and put his head in his hooves. His meal was a little miniature trough full of garbage and banana peels and stuff. I couldn't eat a lunch like that on the best of days.

"What if I told you I had some of my mom's mutton?" I asked, reaching into my lunchbox. Suddenly, Kevin didn't look so sick.

"Well, I . . . if you . . . Okay. Perhaps I could choke down a bit of . . . I think I could do that."

I handed him the mutton, and my timid little friend tore into that leg of lamb like he was a velociraptor. I pulled out the rest of what my mother had packed—a plastic bag full of mung beetles and a Tupperware container holding three field mice. Before you judge me too harshly, remember that I am a troll, and trolls are carnivores. Sorry. Also, field mice happen to be delicious. Especially with some ranch dressing to dip them in. Besides, while I was eating the beetles, one of the mice opened one eye, saw that the coast was clear, and took off like a shot.

He must have just been napping when my mom found him.

Suddenly without a main course, I made my way to the cafeteria line to see what Ms. Locks had on the menu. Nine times out of ten, it was porridge and homemade bread. Ms. Locks and I even had a little porridge ritual. Every time, I'd get up there and ask her, all innocent like, "How's the porridge today? Too hot? Too cold?"

And she'd answer me back in her gruffest lunch lady voice.

She always acted all angry about it, but then I'd catch her giggling as I walked away. A few times she'd caught my eye and given me a wink too. I liked it, 'cause a lot of the kids were scared of her. Ms. Locks is not a small woman, and she's once or twice threatened to sit on kids if they didn't behave. She's apparently a pretty serious bear hunter, and there was even a rumor that she was a witch.

I doubted the witch part, and thought she might have started the rumor herself just to keep kids in line. So I let her growl at me, but it was our little running joke.

Today as I reached the end of the line, she leaned over and caught me by the shoulder. "OH, YOU'RE IN TROUBLE TODAY!" she announced in a loud voice so the other kids could hear. She pulled me around the corner into the kitchen, behind the cauldrons. Then she leaned in with a concerned smile. "You all right?"

I was caught off guard. "What? Oh. 'Cause of the joust?"

"Yeah. I heard about it. You ever been in a joust?"

"Well, no."

"Listen, get there early. And make sure you get to choose your own Swampfrog. If you're gonna win, you need a sturdy frog. Don't let the prince decide."

"Okay." I was looking around, wanting to get back to Kevin and Chester. Nothing could destroy a kid's reputation faster than being seen hanging out with the lunch lady. Not that I really had a reputation to destroy.

"And don't let that little turd give you any trouble, okay?" She gave me a shake. "If he does, you tell him to come talk to Goldie, all right? I was babysitting his daddy the king back when he was still in diapers."

PBBLFTT

She gave me one last meaningful look before letting me go.

I backed out of the kitchen rubbing my arm. "Thanks . . . I think?"

When I got back to the table, it looked like a minor mutton massacre had taken place. Kevin was sitting there holding a gnarled bone, sullenly picking his teeth.

WHAT?

Chester sat across from him intently studying a book of old jokes. He was so absorbed in his studies, he was unaware that a big gooey piece of meat was stuck to the side of his jester's cap.

"Now *that*," I told him as I sat down, "is pretty funny."

DEAD TROLL
WALKING

GRUMBLE GRUMBLE GRUMBLE

The rest of the day was spent being pointed at.
A lot of people stared. I heard the term "Stink
Dragons" whispered behind my back a few times.
Altogether just a great way to spend an afternoon.

So after school, with a few hours to kill before the
Big Showdown, Kevin and Chester and I headed
to our favorite hangout spot—the tree house. It's a
short walk, but it felt long because Kevin was spazz-
ing out so badly.

Having a friend who's a World Class Worrier can be bad enough, but when they have an actual, legitimate reason to worry, it's like pouring gas on a fire.

Now, there are a lot of types of trees in which you could build a tree house. You could put one in an elm, an oak . . . maybe even a garbagefig tree, if you don't mind the smell. But of course we weren't that smart. We built ours in a Wishing Tree.

That may sound great, a Wishing Tree, but let me explain. It turns out the Wishing Trees around here don't GRANT wishes. They MAKE wishes. Constantly. And it can get really tiring.

We figured out a while back that if we give our particular tree enough peanut butter, it shuts him up for a while. But we have to put up with his NUM NUM NUM noises and smacking his lips a lot while he eats it. We've all pretty well learned to tune it out.

When we showed up today, the tree started right in with us. "Man, I really wish I wasn't losing my leaves like this. I'm getting bald patches." "Boy, I wish I had a girlfriend." "Man, I wish I could ride a motorcycle." That motorcycle wish was a constant one, though having been stuck in the exact same

spot his whole life, I couldn't blame him for dreaming about moving around a bit.

We loaded him up with a full jar of extra-sticky peanut butter, which usually gives us about forty-five minutes of peace. Then we climbed up through his branches to our rickety old tree house. It creaked and groaned and shifted around a lot, but it was Home Sweet Home.

Chester pulled an enormous bag of Wizard-Os out of his backpack and asked the question of the day:

I had to think about it for a minute. "I guess so. Although I think I'm more nervous about riding the stupid frog than I am about the prince. What if I fall off in front of everybody? You know Sierra'll be there." (We don't need to talk about Sierra. Cute girl. Enough said.)

Kevin let out a quick little whimper. "I think you need to be less worried about damaging your reputation and more worried about damaging your spine. Or your central nervous system!"

I rolled my eyes and lay down on my back, listening to the muted slurping and munching coming from the tree below. I let out a long sigh.

"What's that mean?" Chester asked through a mouth full of cheesy snack puffs.

"It's just something my gramps says. Means it'll all be okay eventually."

We were all quiet for a while, listening to a breeze blow through the leaves. Sometimes those are the best moments with friends. When you all stop yammering for a minute.

Chester pulled out the latest issue of the Knoble Knight comic—a series based on the real-life adventures of a super-brave knight who had died in battle a few years back.

Chester was obsessed with the knight. I know for a fact that most of his underwear are Knoble Knight–themed. I also know that if he weren't destined to be a court jester, his dream would be to go to knight school.

The three of us just hung out for a while. We played gin rummy with a deck of bikini-maiden cards we kept hidden in a hole in the tree. Kevin and I listened to some truly awful Rapunzel jokes that Chester was working on. I got the high score on Angry Dragons on my phone.

We just killed time until there was no more time to kill. Then we headed off to the joust.

· 9 ·

FROG ON
YOUR THROAT

I'll admit I was shocked by the size of the crowd that had gathered behind the gym. By the time we got there, it seemed like half of the school was milling around. A few of the artsier students had silk-screened some joust T-shirts and were loudly selling them.

They were all standing just off of the athletic field, close enough to the building that they couldn't be seen by any teachers heading to their cars in the parking lot.

Everyone noticed us approaching and grew silent. The crowd parted to reveal Prince Roquefort and his ogres leaning against an elaborately decorated wagon. One from the king's personal collection, obviously. Sitting atop the wagon was a large cage, containing four irritated-looking Swampfrogs.

"So you didn't wuss out after all," the prince said in a voice like nails on a chalkboard. His eyes were at half-mast, giving him a look both sinister and dim-witted.

Okay . . . mostly just dim-witted.

"No, no. I'm all in, Your Splendif-erousness," I said as I bowed sarcastically, hearing a little nervous squeak out of Kevin. I was acting pretty tough, but I'll admit I was nervous. I even had that nervous have-to-pee feeling. Why does your body always want you to go to the bathroom when you get nervous? Maybe it figures there's not too much trouble you can get into in the john.

ALL SAFE IN HERE!

"I've brought four of our best Swampfrogs from the royal stables. Obviously, as I've provided them, you may choose your frog." The prince was really enjoying his role in this. "Fair is fair."

So I approached the cage with Chester and a shivering Kevin close behind me. The ogre that I'm pretty sure wasn't named Buddy opened the door just wide enough for me to reach in and grab a frog. Remembering Ms. Locks's words of advice, I grabbed the largest, meanest-looking one by a horn and pulled. I was unprepared for what happened next.

This stupid Swampfrog bolted like an escaped mental patient. But I held on. I'm not entirely sure why I held on as this insane amphibian jumped around the field smashing my face repeatedly into the ground— but I did. No way was I letting one of the royal Swampfrogs get away. I'd never hear the end of that.

Chester had grabbed a long piece of rope from one of the ogres, and was coming across the field to tie me to the frog—standard practice—when he caught a giant flipper-foot to the jaw.

His jester hat went flying as I heard his teeth slam together, but he kept coming. He dove on us and started looping the rope around me and the frog as best he could.

Kevin was yelling, "Rub its nose! I read it on-line!"

I was completely out of breath. "Frogs don't . . . I don't . . . Frogs don't have noses, do they??" I gasped.

"Then rub where a nose would normally be! It calms them down!"

So Kevin and I frantically rubbed away at its gooey face and—I have to give Kevin full credit here—it worked. After a couple of minutes, the frog was just lying there, purring. Purring! Who knew?

We all lay there for a few moments, gasping for breath. My face was throbbing and my ears were ringing.

I rolled the frog over until I was sitting on its back, the rope tied across my lap. I looked down at my friends, sprawled out on the ground around me. Kevin was whimpering again. Chester's lip was bleeding pretty badly.

THANK YOU, GENTLEMEN. I THINK THAT WENT WELL.

· 10 ·

JOUST THE TWO OF US

I slowly got the feel for riding my Swampfrog. Now that he wasn't completely freaking out, it was only mildly terrifying. So I took my trusty steed on a couple of laps around the goal posts, testing his hops and getting my balance, and then headed back over to the (highly entertained, at this point) crowd.

Sitting there calmly upon his own frog was the prince, with not a hair on his head out of place. He was holding his lance upright and looking all regal. Jerk.

"I have to say, that little show was worth the price of admission all by itself," he smirked.

"Whatever," I said, still considerably out of breath. I felt like I might yarf, but I wasn't going to let anyone else know that. "Let's do this."

So Buddy the ogre handed me my Nerf lance, and the prince and I headed out onto the field. The lance felt good in my hand. It was squishy, but had a firm core. No one would get seriously hurt by one of these, but you could get popped pretty good with a direct blow.

At this point, to my surprise, Chester stepped out onto the field with us, still adjusting his hat and brushing grass off of his tunic. He shouted as he turned to the crowd and raised his hands in the air. "My name is Chester Flintwater and I will be your master of ceremonies for the joust today!"

LADIES AND GERMS!

A groan went through the crowd. Chester was notorious, and not in a good way.

"Before the main event, I thought I would start you all off with a few jokes!" Another loud groan from the crowd.

"Okay. Joke one! You ready? Where does King Cheznott hide his armies? Huh?" No one responded, but Chester was going for it. "Up his sleevies!!"

There was complete silence from the gathered students except for someone in the back who coughed quietly.

HIS "ARMIES" UP HIS "SLEEVIES"! GET IT??

"Arms? Sleeves?" He was visibly deflating at the lack of laughs. "No?" His smile slowly turned into a grimace as if the crowd had disappointed him. "Fine," he said, almost under his breath. "Here's Prince Roquefort and Zarf to . . . you know." He walked off the field dejectedly.

LOUSY NO-JOKE-GETTING SO-AND-SO's...

So Prince Roquefort and I shook hands, which is customary, but it wasn't easy, as he was giving me his shifty little cheese-eating grin the whole time.

"We go to opposite ends of the field, then on the count of three we charge. Yes?" he asked. I agreed and we hopped off to our opposite end zones. My frog was behaving pretty well now, but I rubbed his nose a couple of times just to be safe.

I turned and faced the prince, whose frog was pawing at the ground like a bull ready to charge. I was tense, but ready. Then someone counted to three and it was on. We charged.

POINK

I remember thinking, as the prince and his angry-looking frog grew closer, that I could still turn back. I could just swallow my pride, and refuse to participate in this. Nine out of ten people with a brain will tell you that jousting with the king's son is not a wise move.

But I didn't turn back.

At the last moment, before our lances hit home, I saw the smile on Prince Roquefort's face and knew something was wrong. It looked like the grin of a Mung Beast about to eat a Flack Rabbit.

The prince's lance struck my chest like a nuclear bomb. Pain exploded through my entire body as my frog and I were lifted into the air.

It felt like I'd been shot, or at least like what I think it would feel like. As I hit the ground, with one large, very stunned frog landing on top of me, I blacked out.

I was only out for a second or two. When I came around, I heard a giant sucking sound, and it took a second to realize it was me, straining to pull in a breath of air. Once again, my entire body lit up in pain. I rolled the frog off of me, untying us and sucking in as much air as I could. Lying inches in front of my face was the prince's purple lance, where he had dropped it.

Through the spots flashing in my eyes, I saw Kevin and Chester running toward me. Behind them, the crowd was stunned into silence.

Chester and Kevin righted my frog, which quickly darted off across the field. I was struggling up to my hands and knees when my paw fell on the prince's lance. My dazed brain took a second to register it, but this was no spongy Nerf lance. This thing was hard, solid plastic, with the emphasis on "hard."

Just then, Roquefort slowly hopped by on his

frog. He looked down at me as he passed and smiled his stupid, sneaky, snarky smile.

HEY... I LET YOU CHOOSE YOUR FROG, DIDN'T I?

Have I mentioned before that when I get mad, I see red?

11

LOSING IT, TROLL-STYLE

HUFF.
PUFF.
HRMF.

Well, I saw red then, let me tell you. I felt a big juicy ball of anger making its way up from my toes. I felt my neck flush, followed by my face, and then I . . . well, I kind of lost it. There was an awful growling sound coming from deep in my throat that I had no control over.

I took three running steps and dove at the prince. I drilled into him hard, catching him completely off guard, and we both crashed to the ground.

Before we had even stopped rolling, I started flailing away at him. I felt like I'd been hit by a flaming chariot—and I was completely out of my mind. I don't even know if what I was throwing would be considered punches or slaps, or some stupid-looking combination of the two. But whatever it was, I kept doing it for way too long.

Slowly, my wits started to re-gather in my head and I became aware of the prince, letting out hurt little squawks and grunts and pleading with me to stop. I suddenly realized where—and who—I was. Was I nuts? I stopped my attack and sat back, looking down at the grass-stained prince covering his face. His whimpering was turning into tears. I was still mad, but it was like waking up from a bad dream.

Blinking like someone coming out of a dark cave, I looked around at my fellow students. Everyone stood completely still, including the prince's bodyguard ogres. Even that spazzy kid Aaron, who can never sit still. They all seemed to be in shock. Several mouths hung open, and I saw one elf from my history class pass out—though elves are prone to that kind of thing, of course.

SWOOOON

Suddenly the blood rushed to my face again, but this time it was pumped there by pure shame. Of course, it wasn't the first time I'd gotten angry, but this time was different. I'd never lost control like this. The look of horror on my classmates' faces,

together with the sounds of the prince sobbing be-
neath me, were too much. I knew if I didn't get out
of there, I was going to burst out in tears as well.

So I ran.

As I tore across the field toward my house, I
could feel that hot sting of tears in the back of my
nose. Kevin and Chester were yelling after me. I
turned and shouted at them to leave me alone. I had
never been so disgusted with myself as I was in that
moment. I felt like frog goop.

12

UNDER THE BRIDGE

When I got home, my ribs were throbbing, my head was pounding, and I was bleeding from a number of scrapes and cuts. The athletic field is infested with dragon grass, and that stuff can dice you up like a Cuisinart. I was living proof.

My mom spotted me between the front door and the stairs. She stopped me in my tracks with a loud, concerned mom gasp.

"ZARF! What happened?" She dropped the tiny

duster ferret she was wiping the furniture with and came running. The ferret headed for the hills, leaving little puffs of dust in his wake.

FREEDOM!

I started to tell her a made-up story, but suddenly she was there giving me a hug and I couldn't do it. So I told her. Everything. About the prince, the shoving, the joust, and the fight. About my instant fury. It all just tumbled out of me in a flood while she took me to the bathroom and started cleaning up my scrapes. Then . . . she broke out the Troll Putty.

TROLL PUTTY

Troll Putty is nasty. It smells like a sack full of rotten melons and low tide all rolled up into one. It's apparently good for you, as all troll mothers use it, but when applied to a cut, it feels like you're getting flash-fried in a fire bog. The best way to get through it is to scream and thrash around dramatically. Which I did.

OH! SHEEEEE!! TAKE ME NOW, LORD!!

I was still on the floor, remembering how to breathe as the pain slowly calmed down, when I asked my mom what the deal was with my anger.

"That's just your troll blood, Zarfy."

I gave her a look. "Zarf, mom. Not Zarfy. No more Zarfy."

I'd heard about troll blood, of course. A lot of bad behavior had been chalked up to troll blood over the years. It was kind of the go-to answer anytime a troll flew off the handle.

YOU DESTROYED MY VILLAGE AND ATE MY COW!!

SORRY. TROLL BLOOD.

"Yeah, I know, but what does that mean, exactly? I hate it. I don't want it." I was sitting up, blowing on my knee, which seemed to cool the stinging down a bit.

Just then, my gramps waddled into the bathroom doorway. He crossed his arms and leaned against the frame. You could hear the wood groaning against his weight.

"Now, did I hear tha' right? Were you sayin' you hate your own blood? Tha's jus' ridiculous."

I looked away. I didn't really feel like meeting his eyes. "Yeah well, then consider me ridiculous," I mumbled. "I went all Incredible Hulk at school today and everybody looked at me like I belonged in a cage."

ZARF SMASH!

I could see him out of the corner of my eye. He didn't laugh, but he did stand there for a while with a goofy sideways grin on his face. "Are you abou' done patchin' the boy up in here, Beatrice?" he asked.

"Sure am." My mom scratched behind my ear and kissed the top of my head before she stood up from the edge of the tub. "He's all yours."

"Good. Zarf and I're gonna go catch us some dinner."

A few minutes later, the two of us were waist deep in the creek beside our house. Another perk of our home under the bridge was living right next to one of the best fishing holes in the kingdom.

Right there, not ten yards from our front door, we could catch all kinds of fish. Purple Salmon, Blue Gnarleys, big fat Lumpy Snappers . . . Just about any fish you could think of.

What we did was more like "fish-slapping" than fishing. Like what bears do, if you ever watch the Nature Channel. We quietly wait, standing completely still in the water, hoping a fish will think we're a mossy rock or a furry tree. Then, when one swims up to nibble on our legs, we haul off and slap the stuffing out of it. With any luck, it sends one seriously stunned fish flying up onto the grass.

WHAT THE...?

It's a fun way to spend an afternoon—though probably not for the fish.

We'd been quietly staring into the water for about ten minutes when my gramps spoke up.

"See now, yer troll ancestors were fierce warriors."

I looked at him for maybe a split second, and just missed a Blue Gnarley as it darted between my legs.

"Ya ever heard of the Great Troll Uprisin'?"

Gramps took his time when he talked, but he usually didn't speak up unless it was something worth hearing. "Or how abou' the Battle of Grundy Ledge? You know how those fights were won?"

Just then, Gramps lit up and took a huge swing at the water, sending a geyser of water and one thoroughly confused Orange Smoothgill flying up into our yard. "How were they won?" I asked, without taking my eyes off of the water.

"Troll blood. Those battles were won 'cause of tha' very same blood you have pumpin' through your veins. It's your birthright."

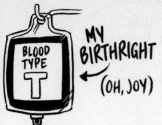

BLOOD TYPE T

MY BIRTHRIGHT (OH, JOY)

"Yeah, well, what if I don't want it?" I asked as I swatted lazily at a leaf that looked a little like a carp.

"Too bad. Yer stuck with it. And unfortunately, yer just abou' the age where it starts ta rear its ugly head. You just have to learn to control it. Channel it and use it for good." He was slowly wading around, looking for a better fishing spot. When I didn't respond, he went on. "Our ancestors used to work themselves into a frenzy before battles. They'd get so fired up, they could chew through rock and swing trees like baseball bats."

RAGE! FURY! DISCONTENT!

He attacked again and another fish landed on the bank with a plop. "So, some of tha' craziness and fury kinda stuck with us over the years. It's been passed down through the generations."

"Yeah," I said, just watching him fish at this point. "That much I figured out. I feel like I'm a ticking time bomb."

"But here's the thing, Zarf. You're a Belford. And us Belfords . . ." He smacked a fish so hard its tail almost fell off. "Us Belfords do e'rything we can ta use our anger ta help others."

Now I was wondering if my gramps had gotten into the Fumpberry brandy a little early today. "That makes no sense."

"It will," he said, pausing to look over at me. "It's sorta the Belford Way, if ya wanna call it tha'." He turned back to the fish.

"The Belford Way," I said aloud.

"Ya have ta look for those moments, and work at it, but you'll see. Yer a Belford, and Belfords lend a hand. My grandda' did it an' his grandda' before him. We have a power, and we have a responsibility ta use tha' power for good."

OH, FOR THE... I'M SPIDER-MAN.

That got my gramps laughing—huge stomach-shaking bellows that shook the bridge above us. "Not exactly. But I know fer a fact yer a Belford."

We fished in silence for a bit while I let that settle in. "Did you get angry a lot when you were younger?"

"Oh, sure I did. Still do! The other day on the square, I tripped o'er a wobble gnome. I got so steamed I chased him for two blocks 'til the little

WHOA.

guy fell down. Then I just kind of felt sorry for him, so I helped him up and bought him a cup o' coffee.

"See, Zarf. You're an evolved, civilized troll with a bloodthirsty hothead troll way down deep inside you. You jus' 'ave to control tha' wild troll anger as much as you can."

I yawned. It had been a long day. "Yeah, I'm not doing real well with that. Any suggestions?"

"Oh . . . The usual. Close your eyes. Count to ten. Walk away for a few minutes. Pet your ears. Rub your belly fur. Even just a few deep breaths can keep you from knocking somebody's block off."

"It's true," someone said from behind me. I turned to find my dad standing on the bank with a couple of towels in his large paw. "It works if you want it to. You just have to keep practicing." He ducked as my gramps knocked another fish his way. "You boys about ready for dinner?"

I waded out of the water and took a towel from him. He put his arm around my shoulders as my grandfather gathered up the fish, and we all headed inside to eat.

·13·

FIRST, THE
BAD NEWS

WHeeZe.
Gasp.

The next morning, I was in my room trying to cram way too many textbooks and moon pies into my backpack when someone started pounding like crazy on our front door. I sprinted down the stairs and threw open the door to find Kevin, looking frazzled and pale like he'd seen a ghost. He was panting and sweating from running all the way from his house.

"Di . . . Did you hear?" He came into the front

hall and collapsed to the floor. He flopped onto his back with his arms spread. "Did you see the paper?" he sputtered, between wheezes. "It's bad."

OH, IT'S REALLY BAD.

I was concerned about whatever his news was, but more worried about his current state. "Kevin, I have no idea what you're talking about. Do you want a glass of water or something?"

"No, let me just . . ." He rolled over onto his stomach. "It's cool here on the tile. Just let me . . . Let me catch my breath." He flattened his cheek against the floor and closed his eyes.

"It's the king! Snuffweasels. He's missing! A bunch of his men."

At this point, my mom came into the entryway. "What was that about the king?"

Kevin took a few more deep breaths and sat up. He blew his nose loudly in a handkerchief and tried to tell the news more calmly. (I know. What kid carries a handkerchief, right? Kevin, that's who.)

SHHNONK

"Okay . . . The king. While we were in school yesterday. He and some of his men went out to hunt down the Snuffweasels. Because of the attack. They were gone all day and all night. They're not back."

My mother tried to find a silver lining. "But that's okay, right? They're probably just still out hunting."

"No!" Kevin was slowly getting to his feet. "No, they aren't answering their phones. The calls go straight to voicemail! It . . . it doesn't look good. Not good at all. This is just . . . Oh, it's so . . ." Then he just tapered off into quiet worried mumbling.

My mom may have summed it up best, in the way only a mother can. "Oh, dear," she said to herself as she headed back to the kitchen.

Kevin fussed and moaned the whole way to school. Not that this was unusual, but it was especially bad that day. Chester was waiting for us outside of the school, at the edge of the Enchanted Field. "You guys heard?"

As soon as we came through the front door, heads started turning in my direction. Lots of heads. A small group of Cheer-Maidens stopped gossiping long enough to turn around and stare as I walked by. It was like I suddenly had three heads.

"What's everybody's problem?" I asked Chester and Kevin in a quiet voice. "Is it just 'cause of the fight yesterday?"

Just then Susan Elvenley, a tall skinny elf (with maybe the biggest braces on her teeth I'd ever seen), stepped right up in my face.

"Aren't you ashamed of yourshelf?" she asked, both saying it AND spraying it. "Beating up on the prinsh while hish father is mishing?" I just stood there, wondering if she was waiting for a response. "You're sho heartlesh." She flipped her bright pink hair in my face as she spun and walked away.

Kevin offered me a fresh handkerchief from his backpack. As I was wiping bits of Susan's breakfast from my face, I looked around at all the staring faces.

"Is that what this is all about?" I asked Kevin and Chester in a whisper. "It's because I hit the prince while his dad was gone? But I had no idea he was missing!"

Kevin had broken into one of his cold sweats. "I don't think that matters now. They think the king might be, ya know . . . dead. People are freaking out. And you kind of knocked the daylights out of his son."

"I think Kevin's right," said Chester, for once not trying to come up with something funny to say. "As much as I can't believe it, I think they feel bad for the little moron."

·14·

ODD
TROLL OUT

I entered the classroom for first period, and immediately noticed that the prince's seat was empty, as were the seats on both sides of his desk, reserved for his guard ogres—Buddy and the other one. As I sat down, the quarterback—one of our larger giants, with the unfortunate name of Swillz—turned around and glared at me. I pretended I didn't see him until he spoke.

WELL, IF IT ISN'T THE FURRY FURY.

I knew he was trying to get under my skin, but I felt a quick flash of pride. The Furry Fury wasn't bad as far as nicknames were concerned. Kind of cool, actually—like some kind of superhero. And certainly better than Stink Dragon.

FEAR NOT, CITIZENS. IT'S... THE FURRY FURY!

But my feeling of pride was short-lived, as more students filed in—each one looking at me more and more like I was some kind of alien specimen under glass. Then Sierra came in (yes, the cute one) and looked over at me with sad, disappointed eyes. That made me feel like taking a nice long jump out of the Detention Tower window.

SIGH.

We were only about ten minutes into our "Knights and the Ladies Who Loved Them" lecture when we heard that familiar pop and blast of static from the PA system. There was some amplified shuffling of papers before the principal spoke.

HELLO, COTSWIN STUDENTS AND FACULTY...

As most of you have heard by now, Notswin's Beloved King Cheznott—along with a small hunting party of our kingdom's finest men—has gone missing. All attempts at contacting the men have gone unanswered, and frankly, the Castle Administration fears the worst.

For that reason, they have released the following Royal Statement:

Citizens of Notswin—

It is with the Heaviest of Hearts that we tell you all

that our Bravest of the Brave King Cheznott has gone missing. Yesterday morn, with his Mighty Sword "Exfoliar" in hand, he set out with three fine men to track and vanquish the dreadful Snuffweasel beasts. That is the last we have heard from them, which is weird, as they are not answering their phones and they usually have good reception, so that really shouldn't be an issue anyway.

At this point, a few heads turned and gave me the stink eye, just in case I wasn't feeling bad enough already.

STINK eye

We are appointing a new king, until such time as King Cheznott might return. It should come as no surprise that the king shall be none other than the Ruggedly Handsome and Thoroughly Awesome Heir to the Throne, Prince Roquefort. We are certain that with his Razor-Sharp Wits and Animal-like Cunning, he will be a perfect replacement for King Cheznott.

ALL HAIL KING ROQUEFORT!!

I felt my heart slide down into my stomach. All of the blood drained out of my face. And if I were a lesser troll, I'm fairly certain I would have wet myself, right there. In a nutshell, MY knuckles were STILL SORE from POUNDING ON THE NEW KING OF OUR KINGDOM!

Every student in my class was turned around gaping at me now. Even Mr. Hirsch was standing there staring at me with his mouth hanging open. His teacher's notes fell out of his hoof and landed noisily on the floor. They all knew it . . . I was one dead troll.

Several people jumped as there was another loud squawk of static from the PA box.

That is the end of the official announcement, but I would just ask that you keep King Cheznott in your thoughts. And long live King Roquefort.

There were a few moments of silence before Principal Haggard spoke up one more time.

And, um . . . On a completely unrelated note, I need to see Zarf Belford in my office immediately.

· 15 ·

OUT OF OFFICE

I stood outside of the school office for a few moments, trying to gather my thoughts. What was about to happen here? Was I going to get yelled at? Detention? A week of detention?? A vision of endless boring afternoons in the tower spread out before me.

HUGE SIGH.

I let out a long slow breath, braced myself, and opened the office door. The secretary, Mrs. Gellar, seemed to jump a bit when she saw me.

"You're here. Yes. Good. I'll tell the principal."

She buzzed him on the intercom, and Principal Haggard appeared almost immediately in the arched doorway to his office.

ZARF. YES. OKAY. THANK YOU FOR COMING.

"Did I have a choice?" I asked as he motioned me into his office with a quick gesture.

"Ha-ha. Yes. Very good. A good point." I wasn't sure what was wrong with him, but the principal seemed both jumpy and really tired as he closed the door and settled in behind his desk.

"Zarf," he started, "I know about the pushing incident in the hall. I know about the joust. And I know you sent the prince, er, the king home with a fat lip and a busted crown." He leaned back in his chair like he wasn't sure what to say next. "And I should punish you . . . I wish I could tell you I was going to give you detention."

Okay. That seemed like a weird thing for him to say. I started to speak, but he cut me off.

"But I can't." He looked away, out of the window, as the rear door to his office slammed open. Standing there grinning were the new king's ogre bodyguards, now dressed head to toe in the ridiculous-looking official uniform of the Royal Castle Guard.

"Zarf, I've been ordered to release you from school . . . indefinitely."

One ogre (I think it was Buddy. Honestly, they're really hard to tell apart) yanked me out of my chair while the other grabbed my wrists and cuffed them behind my back.

CLICK

"You're to be taken directly to Notswin Castle, where a punishment will be doled out for Crimes Against the Kingdom. I have the official orders here, signed by King Roquefort." When both ogres were turned away, the principal looked up at me and quickly mouthed the words "I'm sorry, Zarf."

Everything went black as a burlap sack was thrown over my head. Then they grabbed me under the armpits and dragged me out of the office. Really not a good day so far.

· 16 ·

SUITED AND BOOTED

OOF.
OUCH.

I was thrown roughly into the back of one of the royal flatbed wagons. The road to the castle was paved with cobblestones, and I can tell you I felt every single bump and jostle. With my hands cuffed behind me and a bag over my head, I was tossed around like a floppet gnome in a twister. By the time we crossed the moat, I'd been thoroughly tenderized.

Once we were within the castle walls, I was

hauled from the wagon and swept into a room that absolutely reeked of expensive per-
fume and scented soaps. I smelled serious notes of lavender, grun-
dlewash, and poo-poo berry. It was too much for my troll nose, and I thought for a minute I was going to hurl.

My hood was pulled off (I still don't understand the hood—I mean,
I knew where I was going, right?) and I found myself surrounded by three short women dressed like color-blind clowns. They might have been witches—I wasn't sure. As soon as they saw me, the one with the beehive hairdo let out a disgusted noise.

"Seriously? A troll. My mother, a fine lady, always told me to never touch a troll. Said you'll never get the troll-stink off a' ya, she did." She let out a long shaky breath.

BUT WHATEVER... I'M A PRUH-FESSIONAL.

With that, she held up a garden hose and blasted me in the face. The woman with the curls came at me with a soapy cloth. She scrubbed my face and ears like she was trying to mold them into a different shape.

When she was done, I was blasted again with the water. Then the third woman started in on me with a hair dryer so strong, it made my eyelids flap.

Beehive worked me over with a hairbrush while Curls dried out my ears, shoving

WHZZZZ

~poke.

OW.

actual x-ray

a rag in them so deep, I think she poked my brain.

"Can't have just anyone struttin' in to have a meetin' with the king, we can't." Beehive was now smacking me in the face with a big poofy thing loaded with some sort of powder. "Least of all some mangy troll." She took a handful of another white powder and started rubbing it into my head. "Stand still. This delousin' talc'll take care of any critters ya got on ya."

"Hey!" I said as my sweatshirt was pulled off of me. My shirt was replaced by one with a ruffled collar and a ridiculously ornate jacket. It had so many sequins and baubles, it made my eyes hurt.

IS THIS ALL REALLY NECESSARY?

Beehive cackled like this was the funniest thing she'd ever heard as she wedged a really stupid-looking wig down on my head. She tried to tuck my ears up under it, but they kept flopping out.

"One must be presentable when seein' the king. And frankly, you weren't even close."

The door smashed opened, and my two favorite ogres stepped in.

· 17 ·

His Splendiferousness

The ogres pushed me down the hallway and into one of the biggest rooms I've ever seen. The ceilings were so high a hill giant could have walked around upright without coming close to bumping his head.

I was so overwhelmed that it took me a moment to spot Prince . . . sorry, KING Roquefort sitting at the far end of the room in an oversized throne.

"Hello, Troll."

His feet were sticking straight out like a little kid in his dad's recliner. He was sporting a new, fancier crown and a smug, superior look. I tried to swallow, but my throat had gone as dry as a Twig Witch.

"Come closer, Zoof."

THAT'S CORRECT, RIGHT? ZOOF?

He had a crooked grin slowly spreading across his face. "My name is Zarf. You know that."

"Yes, yes. That's right. Zarf." He tented his fingers together and let out a long, slow breath. It was clear he was savoring this moment. I had the thought that he didn't seem all that torn up about his dad being gone. Seemed to be pretty well pleased with the whole situation. Could he have . . . ?

"Aren't you forgetting something, Zarf?"

I wasn't sure what he was getting at, so I just continued to glare at him. I have a pretty solid glare. I've practiced it in the bathroom mirror a lot.

WHO DO YOU THINK YOU'RE TALKIN' TO?

"I think it's still customary for one to bow to their king, yes? Or have all the laws of decency simply flown out the window?"

I gave him a few more seconds of my glare before I slowly bowed, never taking my eyes off of his.

"Thank you. I think I've earned that, don't you?" he asked. I thought the exact opposite, but held my tongue. "So. Zeef . . . I called you here so you could be the first to hear of some of my new plans as king."

He leaned forward and smiled. This was going to be bad.

"I feel like the time has come to crack down on some of the . . . vermin . . . in this kingdom. The pests." His smile got so wide, I thought it might split his head in half. "I'm talking, of course . . . of trolls."

I felt a kick of anger that almost buckled my knees. Thinking of my gramps's advice about controlling my troll blood, I took a deep breath and let it out as slowly as I could.

"I'll be imposing a series of anti-troll laws in our kingdom. They will be harsh. My real hope is to make things so difficult for trolls that they eventually pack up and leave Notswin altogether."

I reached up and started rubbing my ears and stomach like crazy, trying to stop the troll blood that was bubbling up in my chest and neck.

"First," he went on, "I'll cut all troll wages in half. You are 'lesser creatures,' after all." My face was flushing now. I could feel the heat starting to take over.

"Then . . . there will be limits on how much food trolls can buy. Meat, in particular. Especially mutton, 'cause I hear you all practically live on that stuff." I could feel my pulse pounding in my ears, so I started quietly counting to myself.

"Oh, and this is my absolute favorite . . . Under no circumstances will any troll in this kingdom be allowed to fish. We don't need you all wading in and filthying up our waters, now, do we?"

That did it. I didn't make it past six. Mount Zarfius erupted once again.

It was like a veil of steam dropped over my vision. I was suddenly spitting, fuming, drooling mad, and I must have looked like a well-dressed lunatic. I charged the prince, who just sat there giggling.

I reached the throne, but just as I got my hands around Roquefort's sinister little neck, I was grabbed from behind and jerked backward so hard, I thought my teeth might go flying out of my head.

It was Buddy,

and before I knew it, he had me in a full nelson.

"Ha-ha! Yes!" Roquefort was clapping and kicking his feet in delight. "Thank you!! Thank you so much for losing your stupid troll temper!! I feel like I just got the most wonderful present!" He could not have looked happier. "It's like Christmas, my birthday, and Punch-A-Troll Day all rolled up in one."

I fought against them as the ogres once again cuffed me.

"You just attacked the king of the kingdom in his quarters! I can throw you in prison for as long as I please!"

My heart sank into my stupid furry feet, and the fight drained out of me. Once again, I felt that hot burn of shame as it flooded into my face. Did I seriously have zero self-control?

"You, Zarf Belford, are under arrest in the name of ME!"

(See—I knew he knew my name.)

"I sentence you to as much time in our stinkiest dungeon

as I see fit. Guards? Throw this garbage into the worst hole we have."

I was dragged roughly across the stone floor, but before we left the room, the royal twerp had one more comment.

"I'd get as comfortable as you can in that cell, Troll. It might be a few years before I decide how long you should stay in there."

As I was pulled away, King Roquefort's laughter followed us down the hallway—strange behavior for a kid whose dad was currently on the missing persons list.

· 18 ·

COOL-HAND
ZARF

Now, I'm a troll, but I'm a polite troll, so I won't tell you what awful things the dungeon smelled like as we came upon it.

I started to hold my breath, but realized I was going to be there a while, so I'd better get used to it. The first eighty or ninety breaths were the worst.

A squat little goat was standing guard next to the closely set iron bars of the cell. He pulled a tiny key from his pocket and set to work on an enormous lock. When the door creaked open, I was tossed down a small flight of stairs, where I landed painfully on my butt. The door slammed shut and the room was almost completely dark.

I lay on the damp stone floor and stared at the low ceiling as my eyes adjusted to the dim light. I may have groaned a little. I'm pretty sure I did.

After a bit, I sat up with a loud sigh and turned to take in the rest of the dungeon. I tore off the stupid powdered wig and jacket and threw them in a heap at the bottom of the stairs.

There wasn't much to see because of the gloom.

I got up to walk around the small room. What little light there was came from a few cracks between the rocks of the wall. I was startled to find a few skulls in one corner, but when I accidentally kicked one, it was made of hard plastic—like the cheap ones you'd get at a Halloween store.

FAKE
SKULLS
→

These were probably Roquefort's idea to strike fear in my heart. Near the skulls there was a scarecrow figure hanging from chains on the wall. It had long straw-like hair and realistic-looking ribs showing through its skin. It seemed like the king had gone all out with the set dressing.

I'll admit, I was kind of freaking out at this point. I sat down against the back wall and gnawed at my claws for a bit. Paws and feet, both. It was a bad habit I'd kicked a while back, but now seemed like as good a time as any to get started again.

GNAW
GNAW
CHEW

I started racking my brain coming up with ways to get out of there. Or I should say I tried to come

up with an idea. Eventually my overworked brain
gave out and I slept.

That night was one of the longest of my life. I was
cold and hungry and miserable.

Finally, the morning came, and I heard voices on
the stairs. It was Chester and Ms. Locks. I wasn't
surprised to see Chester, as his family lives in the
castle servants' quarters, but Ms. Locks was a shock.
Especially as she had a Tupperware container full of
biscuits under her arm. I'm not proud of it, but I
may have drooled a bit when I saw them.

Chester told me Kevin had wanted to see me
too, but was turned away at the drawbridge. He'd
seen my family, and had messages from each of
them. Gramps's message had been simply "This

is some Grade A horse pucky." Goldie Locks was only allowed in because she was doing her daily delivery of baked goods and the Royal Meatloaf.

When the guard wasn't looking, Chester slipped me a handful of comic books. "I figured you're probably bored in here." Before I stuck them in my back pocket, I saw they were the latest four issues of the Knoble Knight. I'd been asking to borrow these for a while, but he'd kept "forgetting" to bring them to school. Parting with these was like donating a kidney for him.

Ms. Locks stepped up and opened the Tupperware container.

She took out four biscuits and put them in my hands. "I sweet-talked the guards upstairs into letting me give you a few of these." I thanked her as I

shoved two biscuits into my mouth, crumbs flying.
I jammed the other two into my pockets.

"Now listen up," she said as she took my paws in
her hands. "I'll come back and see you when I can."
She kept looking over nervously at the guard—a
different goat now, as there must have been a shift
change. Then she took the last biscuit out of the
container and placed it in my hands, wrapping my
fingers around it.

"Zarf," she said,
lowering her voice
and looking me
directly in the eye.
"I hope that in this
biscuit, you'll find
a little TASTE of
FREEDOM."

She was slowly nodding at me in a way that was kind of creeping me out.

"Do you hear what I'm saying?" She squeezed my paws. "I hope this biscuit will UNLOCK your memories of being FREE."

Okay, now she was just acting weird. I thanked her again, but had to sort of tug my hands away with the biscuit. The guard told them it was time to leave. They each gave me a through-the-bars-hug and left. But not before Ms. Locks gave me another creepy bug-eyed stare—looking from me to the biscuit and back again.

I wasn't sure what was wrong with her. I thought it might be indigestion or something.

RIDING
THE RAP

SCRAPE
scrape.
.SCRAPE

I took my biscuits and went to the back wall. I decided that tunneling out was my only real option, and there was no time like the present. I was just starting to scrape away at the mortar with my big toe claw when a creaky voice spoke up from just to my left.

"You think you . . . could share one of those?"

I freaked. I jumped about a foot off of the floor and all of my fur stood on end. It's possible that I screamed like a sissylizard, but fortunately there is no video evidence of said scream.

I scrambled away as fast as I could, my heart slamming away in my chest like a Speed Dragon on Red Bull.

I squinted my eyes, looking around for the source of the voice. All

I could make out were those stupid fake skulls and that scarecrow hanging on the wall.

"Who's there? Who said that?"

(Troll Kwan Do isn't actually a thing, but I was desperate, okay?)

Everything was still for a moment before I saw the scarecrow's head move. I felt dragonbumps break out over my entire body. (Dragonbumps eat goosebumps for breakfast.)

With a quiet rustle, the head moved up until I saw a very real eye looking back at me. A sad grin slid across its face, though it was mostly covered by a filthy, shaggy, beard.

"I . . . haven't had a bite to eat for several days," he rasped.

"You're . . ." I sputtered. "You're real??"

My heart was galloping like a royal palomino as I crept up to him. I reached out and poked his arm. Sure enough, it was warm.

"Quite real," he croaked, which brought on a coughing spasm that shook his entire body and left his chains rattling.

My family had known plenty of hard times over the years, so I was all too familiar with the misery of being hungry. I scrambled to get a biscuit out of my pocket and held it up to his mouth. He ate it greedily, grunting with pleasure like . . . well, like a guy who's been chained to a wall without food for a long time, actually.

He asked me to scoop up some water from a shallow puddle on the other side of the cell. I was able to carry enough in my paws so that he could at least wash down the biscuit. Gross, but effective.

It's funny, as I watched him washing down that biscuit, I felt . . . really good. I was picturing my gramps saying "Belfords lend a hand" and felt a quick rush of pride.

"I," the prisoner said as he let his head hang again, "am forever at your service, sir. What do they call you?"

"I'm John. I honestly cannot thank you enough, Mr. Zarf."

"It's just Zarf," I said, digging another wadded-up biscuit out of my pocket. "You want another one?"

"Ah. I would, Zarf, but I fear I might toss my

proverbial cookies. I haven't had more than a few bites at a time for quite a while."

I stuffed the biscuit back in my pocket and moved back to my spot on the wall.

"What are you in for?" I asked, and had to stifle a nervous laugh. It sounded like a line from a movie. This whole thing was feeling pretty unreal.

"Let's just say I got crosswise with the administration."

HOW ABOUT YOU, MY NEW FRIEND?

I told John about my run-ins with Prince-now-King Roquefort. He seemed genuinely concerned when he heard about the missing King Cheznott.

"That's a horrible thing to hear. He's a wonderful king."

That kind of threw me. "Wait. Isn't he the one that tossed you in here?"

"Oh, not the king. One of his advisors. I have reason to believe the king doesn't know I'm down here. In fact, I think he believes me dead."

"He's the king! Shouldn't he know who's rotting away in his . . ."

"There are things he has done, things I alone know. Not to mention the wonderful things he's done for you and your fellow trolls. Trust me when I say he is a good man. The very best, in fact. If he is gone, I fear for what will become of our kingdom."

I thought of a Notswin ruled permanently by Roquefort and felt queasy.

We talked for a while until I thought he'd fallen asleep. I picked up one of Chester's comics and was trying to read by a crack of light when he spoke up. His voice was so raspy, I almost didn't hear it. "What's that you've got there?"

I walked over and held the comic book up in front of him.

THE KNOBLE KNIGHT. THIS ONE'S REALLY GOOD.

At this, the prisoner let out a slow, sad laugh that led into another coughing fit. When he calmed back down, I thought I heard him say under his breath, "That's . . . just perfect."

A few hours later, I bit into that last biscuit of Goldie's, and the pain was like biting into a high-voltage wire.

KEE-RUNCH

There was something rock-hard in there. How I didn't destroy my teeth or my jaw, I'll never know.

I reached into my mouth and pulled out a small key. I was in so much pain that my first reaction was anger at how careless Ms. Locks was to let a key fall into her biscuit dough. (As I've said before, trolls are not the sharpest swords in the weapon shed.)

Finally the pain got down to a dull roar, and I remembered my weird exchange with Goldie. The gears in my stupid troll brain finally sputtered to life and I realized what I had in my hand. Unless it was some cruel joke, it had to be the key to the cell.

GO, GOLDIE!

I jumped up and showed John what I had, and his face lit up like a piece of gleamnugget from the Glimmer Mines.

"Oh. Oh, Zarf. Can you try them on my shackles?" I got kind of embarrassed for a second when I realized he had tears standing in his eyes.

"Sure!" I moved to unlock him, checking that the guard couldn't see us from his station. Then I paused. "Wait. You're not some lunatic who's going to murder me as soon as you're free, are you?"

"Good enough for me," I said, and I slipped the key into the lock on one of his wrists. But hard as I tried, the key wouldn't turn.

"It must just be for the cell door." I felt terrible as John lowered his head, defeated.

I started to pace, but had only gone a few feet when I stopped.

I walked over, got a good grip on one of his cuffs and pried it open, the rusted metal hinge groaning. John fell from the wall, now held up by only one arm. "Troll strength," I explained.

I pulled open the other cuff and he crumpled to the floor. "Sometimes I forget I have it."

John had been hanging there for so long he wasn't able to lift himself, so I grabbed him under his incredibly ripe underarms and pulled him up. I leaned him against the wall as best I could, where he closed his eyes and let out the longest sigh I've ever heard.

LITTLE HELP?

THANK YOU, YOU MAGNIFICENT TROLL, YOU.

I paused, thinking it might be the first time I'd ever heard the words "magnificent" and "troll" put together like that. I kind of liked this hairy skeleton.

·20·

THE GREAT
ESCAPE

RETCH~

For the next couple of hours, John and I put our heads together and came up with a plan. (Actually, I made sure our heads didn't come anywhere close to touching. I think he could have used some of that delousing talc. I saw things moving in that big tangle of hair more than once. So nasty.)

So, once night fell, I casually made my way over to the bars of the cell, coughing and hacking up a storm. I made a pretty good show of it, sniffing and snortling. Wiping my nose on my arm. I won't say I deserve an Oscar, but I think my performance was pretty believable.

It's a well-known fact that goats are germaphobes. For example, you will never get one to shake your hand—it's hoof bumps all the way for them. And if you ever need some Purell or a wet nap, find a goat. Which I realize is weird, as they also eat garbage.

So I called the goat guard over to the bars and told him I thought I was coming down with something. He immediately looked concerned and backed up a foot or two.

OKAYYYY...

"What do you want me to do about it?" he bleated warily.

"I was hoping you could get me a . . . a . . . ahh . . ." And that's when I totally let him have it. The grossest, most explosive fake sneeze I could muster. And I made sure to spray him, but good.

The guard froze as spittle and little bits of porridge biscuit rained down all over him. I actually felt kind of bad as all the color drained out of his horns. He started making little huffs and puffs like he was going to hyperventilate, and then turned and ran up the stairs as fast as his hooves could carry him.

BAAA!

I immediately reached around and unlocked the cell door, swinging it wide open. I ran back and helped John to his feet. He teetered and swayed like a newborn wobble gnome while I threw on the fancy royal jacket and powdered wig. We tried for a while to get John's legs to move—first his knees would knock together, then swing out wide, then he'd collapse against me—before we realized it wasn't happening. So I threw him over my shoulders in a fireman's carry and bolted for freedom. Score another one for troll strength!

The hallway at the top of the stairs was empty, so I picked a direction at random. I ripped the first tapestry I could find off of a wall—a huge, heavy piece of fabric—and rolled John up in it like a big shaggy burrito. Then, hefting him back over my shoulder, I wound through a maze-like series of corridors. At one point we passed an incredibly large lady-in-waiting coming out of a dining hall. She gave me a funny look, so I had to improvise.

TAPESTRY DELIVERY! NOTHING TO SEE HERE!

Rounding another corner, I saw a door that looked like it led outside. I was running toward it as quietly as I could when I heard it. Roquefort's voice.

PARDON ME!!

I froze. Were we busted? But then the prince/king went on, clearly chewing out an underling. "Do you call these underpants soft?? I'm the king! I should not be chafing! Ever!!"

I stifled a laugh and made for the door. When it swung open, we came out behind the castle on a loading dock. Some sort of service entrance. Two rough-looking pigs were sitting on a stack of pallets having a smoke break. One of them gave me a hard stare and flicked his cigarette in my direction.

I smiled weakly and walked past them. Then, as soon as I was around the Dumpster where they couldn't see me, I ran as fast as I could for the woods.

·21·

SANCTUARY

It was close to midnight by the time we got to the tree house, and I was a hot mess. I laid John down as carefully as I could on the ground and started to unroll him. The commotion woke the Wishing Tree, who immediately started up with the wishes.

"I wish I was a deeper sleeper." "I wish I had a midnight snack or something."

I WISH OREOS WERE SO FATTENIN

I collapsed there on the ground for maybe an hour. I didn't have to worry about falling asleep—my mind was racing a mile a minute. Or, as my gramps would say, "my Brain Hamsters were a-goin."

After maybe a half an hour, I got up and told John I was going to go take care of a few things.

"I'm going to cover you up with some leaves and twigs and stuff so you're less noticeable, but I'll be back before the sun comes up. You okay with that?"

John smiled. "Camouflage away. I look kind of like a big hairy stick these days anyway."

I woke up the next morning to John's voice calling my name. The sun seemed like it had been up for a while. I was *reeeally* tired, and my eyes felt like two swollen sand toads.

"Zarf! ZARF!" he was whispering, as loud as he could. "There's somebody coming!"

That jolted me awake. While I had slept in the tree house, we'd had no choice but to leave John on the ground—right out in the open where anyone could see him. I grabbed the binoculars and snake-crawled out onto the tree house landing to survey the area.

I heard the squeaky wheels of Kevin's old red wagon before I saw them. Then Chester and Kevin came around a stand of bushes. Kevin was pulling the overloaded wagon and constantly looking over his shoulder. Chester had a couple of large bags in his arms, but managed to give me a big wave when he spotted me.

The guys had come through for us, and from the looks of that wagon, they'd come through big-time.

"It's okay, John," I said as I swung out and dropped awkwardly to the ground. "They're my friends. They've come to help."

I had tried to go by my house the night before, but it was being watched by several of Roquefort's ogres. They had tried to disguise themselves as shrubs, but I had been able to make them out.

NOT A SHRUB

So I'd gone on to Kevin's house—giving him a near panic attack when I chucked a rock at his window—and asked for the guys' help.

I introduced John to the guys, who were nice enough but understandably gave this human mess of hair and bones a few wary looks. Then we unloaded the wagon.

Kevin and Chester had put together a small feast for me and John, and we immediately dug in. I was a little shocked by John, who tore into that food like he was in the Annual Dragon-Dog-Eating Contest at the Notswin Fair. I guess he was feeling a little better. There was flumpmeat pie, an impressive array of smelly cheeses and fruit, some sort of mutton-based trail mix (Kevin's), a jar of non-alcoholic mead, and enough pastries to fill a minivan. We even fed some of the cheese to the tree, who appreciated it for maybe a minute before starting up again.

OH, I WISH I COULD HAVE MORE. I DO WISH I HAD TASTE BUDS.

While John was still going at it, I helped unload some of the other supplies. Chester had managed to sneak my hoodie and phone out of the evidence room in the castle. He said it was no big deal, because the flying monkey who guarded the room slept most of the time anyway.

I carried a bucket down to a small stream, and brought up enough water for John to shave. He started trying to comb out the messy tangle of his hair, but eventually gave up and moved on to his beard.

Kevin, Chester, and I were sitting on a large log watching John as he began to shave, using a mirror and razor the guys had brought. Chester turned to me and sheepishly asked the burning question on his mind.

SO... HEYYYYY.

"Did you happen to get out of there with my Knoble Knight comics?"

I turned to him, not believing my ears.

SERIOUSLY?

"No, Chester. I had other things on my mind. Maybe if I had an extra hand growing out of my butt, I could have gotten around to . . . "

And that's when Kevin gasped. A loud, sharp gasp, like the time he found a spit-worm in his sock. Chester and I turned to see what he was staring at, all buggy-eyed.

John had now scraped off the majority of his beard, and what was underneath caused all of our jaws to drop.

Sitting in front of us, propped weakly against the Wishing Tree, wasn't John the prisoner. Not anymore. Now it was clear that this man was John Myth. THE John Myth. The Knoble Knight himself.

The one who the comics were based on. We'd seen his pictures so many times in books, there was no mistaking him.

"You're . . ." I gawked. "You're him! You're you!"

The Knoble Knight smiled crookedly as he swished his razor around in the sudsy bucket.

"Well, I used to be."

LEGENDS OF THE
FALL AND RISE

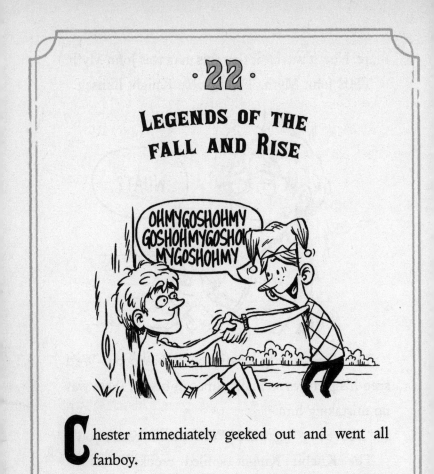

Chester immediately geeked out and went all fanboy.

"Can . . . Can I get your autograph I mean after you get done and we find a Sharpie and maybe I find a copy of one of the comics and you could sign it to me Chester 'cause I think you are the greatest thing since ever and oh my gosh it's so cool to meet you I thought you were dead!" He had run over and was shaking the knight's hand wildly.

Kevin finally found his voice. "But . . . We all thought you died in the dragon battle at Snuff's Pillow Mountain! It was in the paper! It's in our textbooks!!"

The NOTSWIN TIMES
SNUFFED OUT AT SNUFF'S PILLOW
KNOBLE KNIGHT DEAD BY DRAGON

John freed his hand from Chester's death-grip. "Not dead. But I might as well have been. I've been chained up in that disgusting hole ever since. It's a wonder I can lift my arms at all."

I was horrified. "But how did you end up in prison if it wasn't King Cheznott?"

"Well . . . are you all familiar with his chief war advisor?"

"Pembrook. Sure. I know him," Chester said. He knew most everyone up at the castle through his dad. "Big tubby guy with poofy hair."

The knight grinned, looking away. "Let's just say Pembrook's girlfriend . . . She took a liking to me. Very much so."

CAN I HELP IT IF I'M CHARMING?

"So?" I asked.

"So nothing! I never would have gone out with her. I respect the man code. I mean, noble is right there in my name! Or *knoble*, at least."

He sighed, looking off. "But that didn't matter. Pembrook felt threatened, and he and his private goons pulled me out of my tent in the middle of the night."

He stuffed a puffberry muffin into his mouth. "And the rest, as they say . . . is history," he said through a mouthful of dough, crumbs flying. "If I can give you all a bit of advice, avoid small-minded men with any sort of power."

I thought of Roquefort, standing on his throne.

WHAT ARE YOU LOOKING AT?

pea brain

Everyone looked around at each other for a bit before I cleared my throat and spoke up.

"I've been thinking about this. Right now, John and I are probably, like, Public Enemies Number One and Two. Roquefort and this Pembrook guy are going to want our heads on a platter."

Kevin let out a little groan and looked like he might faint.

"So, what if we flipped the script on them? What if we turned ourselves into heroes?" This was met by another little whimper from Kevin.

Chester made a grimace. "I'm listening. But John already IS a hero—lot of good it did him."

"I know, I know. So we do something nobody can ignore . . . something epic . . ."

Kevin and Chester were just giving me a blank stare, waiting.

I leaned in and whispered to emphasize the incredible awesomeness of my idea.

And that's when Kevin really did pass out.

Chester spoke up first. "Wait. We don't even know if the king is alive."

"Right! So that means we also don't know that he's NOT alive." I'd been running this over in my tiny, overworked troll brain since we got out of the dungeon.

I'M DOING THE BEST I CAN!!

"It may be a long shot, but I think it's our best chance of coming out on top. We take out a few Snuffweasels, save the Good King Cheznott and TA-DAH! John and I are back on top again, right?"

I looked over at John, but he was just staring off into the woods, deep in thought.

Kevin was slowly coming to. He sat up and put his head between his knees.

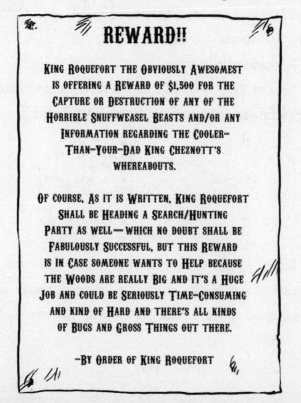

After a couple of minutes, he sat back. "Okay. I'm . . . I'm okay." He turned to me with a heavy sigh, looking like he regretted what he was about to say. "Zarf, I wasn't going to mention this before."

He reached into his back pocket and pulled out a folded piece of paper. "It's a notice from the castle. They're up all over town." He unfolded it and handed it to me, his hoof still shaking a bit.

REWARD!!

KING ROQUEFORT THE OBVIOUSLY AWESOMEST IS OFFERING A REWARD OF $1,500 FOR THE CAPTURE OR DESTRUCTION OF ANY OF THE HORRIBLE SNUFFWEASEL BEASTS AND/OR ANY INFORMATION REGARDING THE COOLER-THAN-YOUR-DAD KING CHEZNOTT'S WHEREABOUTS.

OF COURSE, AS IT IS WRITTEN, KING ROQUEFORT SHALL BE HEADING A SEARCH/HUNTING PARTY AS WELL — WHICH NO DOUBT SHALL BE FABULOUSLY SUCCESSFUL, BUT THIS REWARD IS IN CASE SOMEONE WANTS TO HELP BECAUSE THE WOODS ARE REALLY BIG AND IT'S A HUGE JOB AND COULD BE SERIOUSLY TIME-CONSUMING AND KIND OF HARD AND THERE'S ALL KINDS OF BUGS AND GROSS THINGS OUT THERE.

—BY ORDER OF KING ROQUEFORT

"Fifteen hundred dollars???" I gasped, staring at the piece of paper. I felt the fur on the back of my neck stand up.

THAT'S MORE THAN MY DAD MAKES IN A **YEAR** ON THE DOCKS!

I was stunned. "Well, now we have to do this! It's like it's . . . destiny or something!! Who's in??"

I looked at Kevin, then Chester—and they each avoided my eyes, looking at the ground, or just away into the woods.

I couldn't believe it.

"Seriously, guys?" I looked to Kevin and Chester. They finally met my eyes, looking all sheepish.

SHEEPISH

Kevin spoke first, but in a timid little voice. "Look, Zarf. I'd do anything for you. You're my best friend in the world. No offense, Chester."

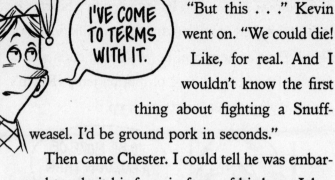

"But this . . ." Kevin went on. "We could die! Like, for real. And I wouldn't know the first thing about fighting a Snuff-weasel. I'd be ground pork in seconds."

Then came Chester. I could tell he was embarrassed to admit his fears in front of his hero, John.

"I mean, I love a good battle and all . . . but this is serious stuff we're talking about."

We all sat there in silence for a while, listening to some tree gnomes singing a working song way off in the distance. Something about tiny hands making big progress.

Finally, it was John who broke the silence. "Zarf," he croaked, his voice still sounding like chains being dragged over gravel. "I'd go with you in a heartbeat. But I can barely stand up, much less walk or run or fight." Even as he spoke, he was doing curls with a couple of half-pound bags of mutton jerky (Kevin's again), trying to get his strength up.

I'D BE MORE OF A BURDEN THAN A HELP.

We all lowered our heads. I was picking sullenly at a blade of grass.

"But . . ." he said. And there was something in the way he said it that made us all lift our heads. "That doesn't mean I couldn't train you."

I glanced over at Chester, who had a look of wonder on his face like a kid who was just told he could be quarterback in the next Dragon Bowl.

YAYYYY!

"Seriously?" he asked, and I could almost see his heart start to beat faster.

"Sure." John pushed himself up a little taller against the tree. "And I could  tell you guys how to get into my house so you could get my weapons."

"Yeah??" Chester was starting to get to his feet, despite himself. Kevin was looking quickly from one of us to the other, unsure what was happening.

"Sure! Yeah!" John was getting excited too. "I could make you guys a fighting force to be feared in a couple of days!! Or, at least, you know . . . not sitting ducks. You can take me along in that wagon of yours in case I get some strength back."

I was on my feet. "Yeah, of course! Go on."

Chester was all in at this point. "Can I use a sword? I always wanted a sword!!"

"Absolutely!" John was getting into full Knoble Knight mode now, firing up his troops. There was a commanding growl in his voice that I hadn't heard before. "And Kevin!"

Kevin jumped a little at the sound of his name.

"Kevin. Give me a couple of days and I'll make you a warrior."

AT LEAST... KIND OF.

"Kevin the Invincible!" Kevin was slowly coming to his feet now too. He was liking this. "Men will want to be you and women will want to date you."

Kevin's eyes grew at this. "Even . . . even Meredith, the cute girl who works the counter at the butcher shop??"

"Even Meredith, Kevin. Even Meredith." John leaned his head back and looked across the three of us, surveying us like new recruits. "Give me two days, and I'll make men of you three." He said it with conviction. "Or, you know . . . as much as I can. More so than now, at any rate."

Kevin was shaking a bit, but he looked from Chester to me to John and finally reared back and yelled.

Which was kind of weird, but okay . . . whatever.

· 23 ·

Forged from Steel

... or Something

If this were a movie, this is where I would drop in a montage of us training for the next couple of days. I'd put it to some inspiring song—maybe "Eye of the Tiger" or an inspirational rap song or something. I'd show us sneaking into the village at night like ninjas and coming away with a wagonload of John's old cool weapons.

I'd cut it together with scenes of Chester learning the fine art of swordplay, and Kevin doing push-

ups, and me running through a tire course and getting the hang of some wicked-looking nunchucks.

I'd show John trying valiantly to get to his feet, but collapsing back against the tree, frustrated.

Then, in that way they do in movies that makes everybody feel kind of weepy, I'd drop the music down real low and show me writing a note to my family on the back of the reward notice.

Dear Mom and Dad
AND Gramps,
It's me, Zarf. I'm okay. I can't
come around the house cause
there are ogres in the bushes.
Seriously.
I know you're worried, but
I'm taking care of things. It's
the Belford Way, right? I'm
super mad, but I have it
under control—sort of.
I miss you guys so much.
I'll be home soon. Catch some
big fish for me, Gramps.
Love you all,
Zarfy

Then I'd show Kevin stopping by to see my parents and slipping the note into my mom's pocket when he hugged her good-bye.

You'd see Kevin telling his folks that he was going to stay the weekend with Chester. And Chester telling his dad that he'd be camping for the weekend with Kevin.

YESSIR. JUST YOUR USUAL, NORMAL, BORING OLD BACKYARD CAMPING.

Finally the music would taper off as you see the four of us sitting under the tree at sunset, eating and talking and loading our packs.

All of that would be really cool if this were a movie, but it isn't, so let me get back to it . . .

"Okay, okay. One more." Chester had been telling us a series of knock-knock jokes, each one worse than the one before.

"Knock, knock."

We all obliged. "Who's there?"

"Thumping."

"Thumping who?

THUMPING BIG AND HAIRY IS CREEPING UP BEHIND YOU!

We all groaned, but I did see Kevin steal a quick look over his shoulder, just to be sure.

"Listen." John's smile slowly faded. "If we meet up with something big and hairy with fangs, like a Snuffweasel, you have to use your strengths. Repeat after me: Use Your Strengths."

We all mumbled it back to him.

Kevin shoved some mutton jerky into his mouth.

"What if your particular set of strengths are kind of stupid?"

John: "Nobody's strengths are stupid."

We all sat there for a few minutes while that sank in.

"Listen. I think you guys are ready," John said, before sinking his teeth into a big flumpfruit.

REALLY?

"Well," John spoke through a mouth full of flump. "I mean, ideally I'd have another couple of years to whip you into shape. But sure, two days is good too. I think we can do this. It makes me sick that I can't help out more, but I'll be there every step of the way."

Just the day before, John had tried to show us that he could get up and around. He'd gotten shakily to his knees before he took a massive digger into the rocky ground. His face was all scraped up and he had two wadded-up tissues sticking out of his nostrils.

"You guys have shown real heart." He looked off at the sunset for a minute. "This journey is deadly serious. We'll have to face some of our fears. Like that awful Snarly Tangle and the horrible things that reside in there. But I feel it in my bones that we'll do okay and make it all the way to the shores of the Sea of Tomorrow if we stick together. If I didn't believe that, I'd say we shouldn't go."

The day before, John had drawn up a map of our journey.

In his solo travels, he said he had once stumbled upon what had to be the main lair of the Snuffweasels. Nestled in a hill on the shore of that famous sea.

John lowered his voice as he spoke, even though there was no one but us around. "I guarantee you most of the search parties will head for the Glimmer Mines. People seem to think those mines are Snuffweasel central. But I'm here to tell you they're wrong.

"Now," he went on, his rough voice cracking just a bit, "you all need to get some sleep, because you don't want to enter the Tangle if you're not fully alert. Trust me on that."

We did.

So we slept. Or tried to.

· 24 ·
OUTTA THERE

FORWARD HO!

The next morning, as the sun started to lighten up the sky, we loaded John into the wagon and headed off into the woods.

The problem became apparent almost immediately. Every time the wagon rolled over a tree root or a rock (and there were a lot of them), John would fall out. He just didn't have the strength to hold himself upright. We tried it ten or twelve times, while John got more and more frustrated, before we tied him to the wagon. But even that didn't work.

I pulled Kevin and Chester aside for a serious talk. Every once in a while, John would yell at us from his spot on the ground.

"I know what you're talking about!!" He was getting really irritated, but couldn't even sit up at this point. "You're not going without me! I absolutely forbid it!"

Finally, we came back and told John our decision. He was furious as I carried him back to the Wishing Tree, thanking him all the way for everything he'd done to prepare us.

Eventually, he saw that our minds were made up, and he got all worried and parent-y.

"You guys . . .

you have to be so careful. I wouldn't be able to live with myself if something happened to you."

We left him some poo-poo berry fritters, a bag of porridge biscuits, a flask of water, and a couple of camouflage blankets.

He shook each of our hands and asked us one more time to stay. But as we walked off, into the woods, he shouted to us.

GODSPEED, YOU MIGHTY WARRIORS!!

We loaded our packs into the wagon and walked for a while in silence. I think Chester and I were just as nervous as Kevin for once. We were making our way through woods we had played in all of our lives, but they looked different now. Spookier. At one point, a tiny tree ferret jumped across our path, and Kevin jumped back so violently, he knocked the wagon over.

We spent a few minutes reloading our supplies while I grumpily explained to Kevin the subtle differences between an eight-inch tree ferret and a seven-foot Snuffweasel.

7 FT. 1 IN.

8 IN.

AVERAGE TREE FERRET

AVERAGE SNUFFWEASEL

About an hour later, we came to a small wooden bridge over a fast-moving stream. Some overly dramatic explorer had dubbed it The Last Chance River, but I knew a stream when I saw one. This was as far from the kingdom as any of us had ever been, because just beyond the stream began the much more dense Snarly Tangle.

Kevin was visibly shaking. "We could still turn back, you know. I mean, I heard there are meat-eating trees in there. Seriously. And leech-bats and maniac gnomes and mosquitos the size of mid-sized sedans."

We all stood staring into the trees for a moment. The way I saw it, this was our first real test.

I'll admit, maybe my teeth were rattling together a bit. I closed my eyes and started taking big, deep breaths. I banged my balled-up paws against the side of my head a few times. Finally, I put my head down and trudged forward, pulling the wagon over the bridge.

"I'm . . . I'm going. You banana heads can come along or go on back."

It took every ounce of strength in me to not look back and see if they were coming.

When I realized Kevin and Chester were once again walking alongside me through the trees, I felt a rush of relief so big, I almost barfed.

· 25 ·

THE SWEET LIFE

The woods were just as dark and scary as I'd expected, and rolling that wagon over all the tree roots was slow going. But on we slogged. At one point, Chester got his tunic snagged on a branch, and there were a few moments of ridiculous screeching and running around in circles.

I think we all thought Chester was a goner. Tree food, for sure. But it turned out it was just a branch.

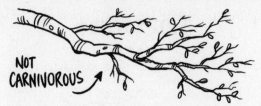

NOT CARNIVOROUS →

At times, we tried humming songs to pass the time, but then we would hear something off in the woods and we'd all get quiet.

A bit later, we stepped into a clearing to find a small house—but it wasn't like any house I'd ever seen before. The entire thing—from the shutters to the walls to the bushes around the place to the quaint little chimney on top, was made of candy and sweets. I kid you not.

We just stood there for a moment, taking it in.

Finally, Chester cleared his throat. "Um . . . do you guys know what has two thumbs and likes to eat candy?"

Internally, I groaned. This joke was older than dirt, but I let him have his moment. "What?"

He reared back and yelled like a lunatic.

THIS GUY!!

And then he was running toward the house, laughing at the top of his lungs.

Kevin took off behind him, in some sort of candy trance.

Do you ever get that feeling, like you should know something, but you just can't remember it? Like when you're trying to think of a word, and it's right on the tip of your stupid tongue?

IT'S RIGHT ON THE TIP OF MY TONGUE.

NO, I THINK THAT'S A PIECE OF CORN.

That's how this felt. A candy house. Deep in the woods. Something seemed way too familiar about this set up.

GUYS!! HOLD UP!

Chester and Kevin turned around, looking annoyed. "What?"

"Nothing strikes you as weird about this? My spidey senses are tingling."

Chester snagged the doorbell and popped it in his mouth.

"Zarf," Chester said, like he was talking to a child, "it's candy! Sweet, delicious, innocent candy!" He plucked a leaf of a gummy shrub and bit off a big chunk.

"Well we should at least see if somebody's home before we eat too much." I stepped up and knocked lightly on the chocolate door. It swung open with a slow creak.

I stepped into the small, darkened house. It was really just one room. There was an unmade bed in one corner and a beat-up old table in the middle. The rest of the room was made up of an impressive kitchen. In one corner there were two large ovens.

Again I had that nagging feeling.

I stepped outside to find Kevin and Chester still eating.

Kevin, being from a construction family, was raving. "I'm really just blown away by the structural integrity. Those must be load-bearing candy canes. It's very impressive."

I pulled off a couple of decorative Tootsie Rolls and popped them in my mouth, but my heart wasn't in it.

"Guys. Something is very wrong here, not to mention the fact that you're destroying someone's home."

Kevin struggled to swallow a big chewy wad of taffy. "I'm the nervous one in our group and even I think you're being kind of a drama queen."

"Yeah. Yeah I guess you're . . ."

And that's when I saw a dark figure approaching through the trees. There wasn't much light in those woods, but it was just enough for me to pick out the unmistakable shape of a witch's hat.

Suddenly all of the pieces started falling into place like a big game of Tetris inside my head.

I couldn't get the words out fast enough. They came out all garbled up.

G...GUYS! WITCH!! HETEL AND GRANSEL!

"It's . . . TRAP!" I was yell-whispering at them, both as loudly and quietly as I could.

Kevin turned to see what I was looking at, annoyed at the distraction.

"What are you yammering about? You mean Hansel and Gretel?" Then his eyes suddenly widened. He jumped up and snorted, making him cough so hard, a big pink glob of taffy shot out of his nose like a rocket, nailing Chester in the ear.

We knew all too well the story of Hansel and Gretel. They were in college now, but their almost-becoming-witch-grub story had been made into a chilling After-School Special that still gave me the willies.

Complete chaos took over for a moment. Finally our feet caught up with our brains and we took off running for the woods behind the house.

* * *

I've always taken pride in my abilities at hide-and-seek. I once hid for an entire afternoon behind a small tree no wider than a piece of string cheese.

I'm convinced hiding is a matter of will. You have to believe with every fiber of your soul that you're invisible, and you will be invisible. (It's also possible that the kids I was playing with that day were just messing with me. Very possible.)

Well, as we all found places to hide, I was willing myself invisible harder than I ever had in my life. I had zero interest in becoming a toasted troll sandwich.

TOASTED TROLL ON A HOAGIE ROLL WITH ARUGULA AND A LIGHT HORSERADISH MAYO.

I ducked into a hollow at the base of a tree and saw Chester and Kevin dive behind a patch of thorny bushes. Then I don't think I took a breath for the next five minutes.

I was just starting to think we'd made it out alive when I heard the loud snap of a twig a few feet away.

"Zarf?"

The voice was kind of familiar, but I thought my best bet was to continue cowering.

Then I felt a hand on my shoulder.

"Have you lost every marble in your head?"

I slowly opened one eye and felt immediate relief flood through my body. It was Ms. Locks, and I had never been so happy to see a lunch lady in my life.

My relief had taken about two seconds to turn into irritation. "What are you doing out here strolling around in a witch's hat??"

"Um, excuse me?" Goldie wasn't one to take any guff. "I'm not the one eating people's weekend cottages, you little weirdo!" Then she swept me up in a bear hug.

At this point, Kevin and Chester came crawling out of the bushes, plucking sharp thorns out of their clothes and hair. Goldie turned to them.

"And what are you halfwits doing out here? I know this one here is on the run from the law, but what's your excuse?"

"Never mind. Let's get you inside and cleaned up. Those snagglethorn scrapes'll get nasty in no time." She shooed us all ahead of her and into her tiny candy house.

As we walked back to her house, I blabbered on and on about how thankful I was for her slipping me the key in jail. She just kind of waved me away and said it was "No biggie."

When we were all gathered around the table, she started pulling Tupperware containers out and setting them before us.

"It's a good thing I showed up when I did or you little jackals would've gnawed this place down to the foundation."

Kevin, still shaking a bit, asked the question on all of our minds.

SOOOOO... GOLDIE?

"Hmm?" Ms. Locks was still bustling around the kitchen.

"Are you—and do pardon me for asking—but are you by any chance the witch that tried to eat Hansel and Gretel?"

Ms. Locks stopped, staring blankly at Kevin. A glob of cinnamon porridge fell to the table from the wooden bowl she was holding. Then she barked out one of her loudest Goldie laughs, shaking the Snickers Bar rafters and startling us all.

"Oh, goodness no," she said, and had to sit down from laughing too hard. She regained her composure and wiped a tear away with the corner of her apron. "Is that why you little grunts were so scared? That's a hoot."

Kevin let out a huge sigh, leaning back in his chair.

MY FRAGILE CONSTITUTION CAN'T TAKE THIS.

Chester spoke through a mouth full of mashed potatoes. "Well, you were wearing a witch's hat. That's kind of weird."

She chuckled. "I just wear that old thing in the woods 'cause of the tree ferrets. I got tired of them bouncing acorns off of my head. Now they roll right off.

"I bought this place from the original owner a few years back, and found the hat. Now, that woman was a piece of work. Mean, cranky old witch. But after the Hansel and Gretel business, she moved down to Cabo and opened a tiki bar, I think."

She sat back and took in the room. "This is my weekend getaway! I got lucky and bought it for a song."

She gave us a sideways wink. "You try buying a second house on a lunch lady salary."

Chester spoke up again as he reached for the yams. "Well . . . the kids at school think you converted to witchdom or something."

A sneaky grin slid across Goldie's face. "Oh, I like that . . . Let's let the twerps keep right on thinking that."

Goldie put us up for the evening in some sleeping bags under the kitchen table.

We woke the next morning to an amazing breakfast of scrambled eggs, bacon (Kevin passed), porridge biscuits, sautéed smooshrooms, and enormous chilled glasses of flumpfruit juice.

When we were so stuffed we could hardly waddle, Goldie walked us out.

"This goes against every fiber of my being, letting you idiots go on like this. But I can see there's no stopping you."

I gave her a quick hug. "Thanks, Goldie. And you'll check on the Knoble Knight?"

"I'm headed there now. So don't you worry about him."

As the three of us headed off into the woods, Goldie called out to us one more time.

BE CAREFUL, YOU LITTLE NIMRODS!

ONWARD HO

SNUFFWEASEL
SNOT

Most of that day went by without any craziness. At one point, we found a crusty, wrinkled-up Snuffweasel handkerchief, which convinced us we were on the right path. (Snuffweasels are known to have terrible allergies.)

We were washing our faces in a small pond that afternoon when we ran into a family with a home in the area. After some discussion amongst themselves, they invited us to their home for a light dinner and a place to sleep.

The dinner and their home were pretty nice, with the small exception of their youngest son, who had a bad habit of crying out "WOLF!" at the top of his lungs every twenty or thirty minutes. For obvious reasons, this did not sit well with Kevin.

The boy's parents assured us that it was just some sort of involuntary tic, but it really took a toll on poor Kevin's nerves. We'd no sooner get Kevin's heart rate back to normal than that kid would let rip with another "WOLF!"

It wasn't until after dinner that the family told me they'd feel more comfortable if I were to sleep outside—being a troll and all. I wish I could say I was horribly offended, but you have to understand that I'd been up against this kind of thing my entire life. And I was just too tired to make a big deal out of it. So, when Kevin and Chester were given fluffy sleeping bags by the fire, I was shown out back to a rusty wheelbarrow with a bag of beans for a pillow. Chester and Kevin protested and said they'd sleep outside with me, but I insisted they sleep by the fire. At least two of us would get a good night's sleep.

But it turns out there was no restful sleep for any of us. The boy continued to scream "WOLF!" in his sleep every hour or so, sending Kevin through the roof. By the time Chester got him calmed back down, it would happen again. When we got on our way the next morning, I think

Kevin was in worse shape than if he'd slept outside with me.

Later that afternoon, we were carefully making our way through a particularly nasty thicket of purple and orange snagglethorn bushes when my phone began to ring.

We all stopped and I dug my phone out of my pocket (suffering a few nasty scratches in the process). It was a number I didn't recognize.

At first I didn't think there was anyone there. I was about to

HELLO?

hang up when I heard some shuffling around and a muffled voice.

"Hello?" Now I could make out a couple of voices, though I couldn't understand them.

Then the line cleared up and I heard a familiar voice complaining.

". . . once and for all that I need a new brand of tights. These keep creeping up my backside! I simply cannot take the wedgies anymore."

I turned to Chester and Kevin, delighted.

"It's Roquefort! He must have butt-dialed us!"

I did, and we all stood grinning like idiots listening to Lord Fumblepants as his phone rustled around in his pocket.

"Not to mention this pair is all snagged and torn from that thicket of snagglethorn bushes we passed through a bit ago."

Chester plucked a tiny piece of royal purple fabric from the bush in front of him and held it up for us to see.

HE WAS JUST HERE!!

One of the ogre bodyguards was talking, but we couldn't make out what he was saying. There was some more fumphering about, and then we heard a blood-curdling growl come through the phone.

WHAT WAS THAT?

I clearly heard one of the ogres yell "RUN!!!" Another voice yelled out what sounded like "BEARS!!!" though it was pretty muffled. There were more growls and the frantic shuffling of fabric against Roquefort's phone. Someone screamed and the phone abruptly went dead.

The three of us were shocked into silence for a moment.

"Did he say bears??" I was hoping I hadn't heard that right.

Chester started shaking his head. "No. No. I'm pretty sure he said 'pears.'"

"Why would he scream 'pears'?" Kevin asked as we both turned to Chester. "And what kind of pears growl like that?"

Kevin's face had gone pale. "No. It was bears."

We all stared blankly at each other for a moment before Chester spoke up.

"Well!" He clapped his hands together. "Easy come, easy go, I always say. Maybe the king can make another prince."

"A nice one this time," Kevin mumbled, looking at the ground.

"Guys . . ." I closed my eyes and sighed, rubbing my face with my paws. "They still have a chance."

Chester looked dumbfounded. "Wha . . . ? Seriously? You want to help them? Roquefort threw you in prison, Zarf! He was gonna leave you there to rot!"

"Right," I said. "And if I never saw him again, it'd be too soon. But I can't just stand here and let him and his ogres get their awful little bones picked clean by bears. OR pears."

THIS IS THAT BELFORD WAY THING AGAIN, ISN'T IT?

Kevin piped up, sounding near panic. "Your gramps didn't say a thing about the Littlepig Way. I'm full-blooded Littlepig, and it's about time for me to go 'wee wee wee wee' all the way home."

"C'mon guys." I almost couldn't believe the words I was saying. Was I really talking about risking our lives for these dopes?

"As much as it pains me to say it, if we don't help them out . . . we're no better than they are."

That got the guys thinking.

"Okay." Chester looked really torn. "I see your point, but I'm not very happy about it."

We both looked at Kevin, questioning.

So we started fighting our way through the bushes again.

"I'm telling you," Chester yelled between huffing and puffing, "it's gonna be pears!"

· 27 ·

THE BEAR FACTS

We heard another growl up ahead of us and followed the sound, leaving the wagon and scrambling through the thick woods with as many weapons as we could carry.

We had stopped to see if we could hear any more growling when a faint groan came from our left. We dashed over to find one of Roquefort's ogre hench-men (Buddy, I'm pretty sure) lying flat on his back next to a tiny creek.

We propped him up against the trunk of a fir tree. He had a knot the size of a stumptoad forming on his forehead.

IT'S A PRETTY NASTY LUMP, BUT I DON'T THINK IT CAN MAKE YOU ANY UGLIER.

"Har-har." He felt his forehead gingerly. "We were ambushed. Scrummel Bears. Mean ones."

With that Kevin and I gave Chester a "See?" look. He shrugged and looked away.

COULDA BEEN PEARS.

Let me say this. Scrummel Bears may be small, but what they lack in height, they make up in sheer meanness and stupidity. Awful things.

HSS. GRR.

FFT. FFT.

"They took King Roquefort and the other guard."
The ogre looked down, ashamed. "I tried to stop 'em."

Kevin spoke up. "Well, don't feel too bad. It looks like one of them got you pretty good."

Buddy seemed to slump down even further. "No. I kind of spazzed out. Ran around a bit."

We were all silent for a moment, letting that sink in.

"Do you have a phone?" he mumbled. "I tried to text Prince . . . I mean King Roquefort, but I can't get reception."

"Really? Who's your provider?" Chester asked him.

"Grimm, unfortunately."

Kevin threw his hands up in disgust. "SEE? Grimm is the worst! I told you guys."

I pulled out my phone—full bars!—and started to hand it to the injured ogre.

"Can you do it?" he said. "My head is pounding like a . . . like a . . . like a pound cake." Which made no sense, but the poor guy HAD just face-planted into a tree.

OGRE-SHAPED DENT →

While I texted, Kevin and Chester explained about the butt-dialing and hearing the attack.

The following is a transcript of the text conversation that took place between Acting-King Roquefort and me:

> Hello? Are you okay?

> Helloooo? Anybody home?

> Who is this? ZARF?? WTH???

> Trying to help here. I'm out of jail and here with your ogre buddy.

> Oh. Oh. When I get out of this mess I'm gonna WWHHOOAA! SAVE ME! HELP ME!!! We're sinking! Honey! So sticky!

Wait. What? Honey? And why would you take the time to type "WWHHOOAA!"?

Focus, Troll! Stop messing about! I command you as your king to come get me out of this! We're in a honey bog! The bears have already gone under!

Fine. But we're having a long talk afterward.

FINE! WHATEVER! Come quickly, Troll! QUICKLY!

How can we find you?

We're . . . Follow the creek and look for an enormous OH NOOO AAUUGH!!!

You still there?

. . . enormous flumpfruit tree. It's just past that!

Seriously. You're just wasting time when you type the noises you're making. It's weird.

Now, Troll! Now!!

The four of us took off, following the almost empty creek bed. Buddy (let's just agree from here out that this was Buddy—I'd have asked him, but at this point it would have been really awkward) was a little shaky on his feet at first, but he kept up. Before long we spotted a gigantic flumpfruit tree, and just beyond it was the honey bog.

I'd never actually seen a honey bog, but I'd heard enough to know they were incredibly dangerous—and tasty. Bog honey is some of the thickest, stickiest honey in the world, and it can make a disgusting flaxseed biscuit taste like heaven. But stumbling into a honey bog makes a struggle with quicksand seem like slipping out of a warm bath. Seriously. Honey bogs scoff at quicksand.

PSSH. WHATEVER.

We ran up to the edge of the bog, careful not to dip even a toe into the goo.

There was a dead tree lying across the bog, and

several feet out, a cage was hooked on one of the branches. It looked like the cage the Swampfrogs had been in at the joust. Inside the cage, whining and cursing like a sticky foul-mouthed baby, was Roquefort—half submerged. There was also some sort of fancy antique chair in there with him, which made no sense to me.

COULD YOU HAVE TAKEN ANY LONGER?

"Get me out of here! It's a delectable trap!!"

Just to the side of the cage, there was a tiny little Scrummel bear claw sticking out of the honey. It wasn't moving. Next to it was the tip of a bear's backside. The Scrummel Bears had not fared well.

Then I spotted the other ogre, or I should say I spotted the very tip of his nose and lips, sticking out of the honey closer to shore. It was a struggle, but he got out a muffled cry for help.

LITTLE HELP HERE?

Buddy started to make his way out onto the dead tree. But his weight was too much, and the tree rolled, forcing Roquefort farther into the sticky mess. Roquefort squealed.

This whole Belford Way thing was proving to be a giant pain.

I made it halfway out on the tree before it rolled again.

EEP.

I swayed, flailed my arms, and swung my hips like I'd invented some new, stupid-looking dance—but I fell in anyway. I sank in slowly, but the parts that went in were stuck. Really stuck.

Being the brain trust that I am, I reached my hand down to pull a foot out—and that hand got stuck. It was like playing Twister in Super Glue.

My friends sprang into action. It was like watching TV on fast forward. Suddenly Chester was up the flumpfruit tree and yanking out the longest vines he could find. Kevin tied one of the vines around his waist and crawled out onto the log, pulling the other vines behind him—with Chester holding the log as still as he could.

Kev dropped the first vine over the mouth of the submerged ogre, who clamped it between his teeth, and then Buddy began pulling with everything he had.

Roquefort saw this and went nuts. "WHA . . . ?? The ogre's DISPOSABLE!! I'm your KING!!"

I DEMAND TO BE SAVED FIRST!!

Kevin stayed focused on his task, and I had a moment to wonder: Could this possibly be my scaredy-pig friend coming to my rescue? Then, as he tossed me a vine, I realized it was all because I was in danger—he hadn't thought twice—and a lump the size of a Lava Dragon lodged itself in my panicked throat. Then I was being pulled to shore as well.

Next, Kevin tied a vine to the rungs of Roquefort's cage, sat back, and kicked the cage free. The force of his kick rolled the tree again, and Kevin flipped. My heart sank as he landed face-first in the honey, with a sound like a pumpkin landing in pudding.

SPLAP!

Chester pulled as hard as he could at Kevin's vine. There was a loud sucking sound as Kev was pulled backward, and his honey-covered face slid free.

"OH! OH, IT'S SO TERRIBLY STICKY!" he gasped.

Then I just held on as hard as I could while Chester and Buddy dragged us all (slowly) out of the mire.

As soon as Kevin was pulled clear of the bog, I rolled over and threw a sticky arm around him. "Thank you, Kevin." We were all gasping for air. "You saved my life." I was getting misty-eyed with emotion. "That was so awesome."

Kevin sat up. "It's okay, Zarf. I . . . Wow. I really did it, huh?"

"You sure did, Kev. That was amazing. You totally risked your life for all of us!"

That was when Kevin started to shake. "I sure did . . . Risk my life, I mean . . . I . . ." He started breathing harder, and a cold sweat broke out across his forehead as it all sank in.

WHAT...
WAS I
THINKING?!?

Kev's eyes were suddenly bugging out of his head, and he started sucking in air in big whooping gulps. "I COULD HAVE DIED!! DEAD DIED!!! HOLY MOLY, I COULD HAVE SMOTHERED IN SWEET, SWEET GOOEY—" And then he abruptly passed out.

Ten minutes later, after Kevin regained consciousness and his wits, we all sludged our way from the edge of the honey bog to the nearby creek, looking like syrupy, leaf-covered swamp monsters. Every fly in the kingdom seemed to have found us as well.

We were sitting in the water, letting the creek slowly wash the honey off of us, when Roquefort turned to look at Kevin.

DOES ANYONE ELSE SMELL HONEY-CURED HAM?

I cut him off. "Enough. We're all exhausted, so give it a rest."

Roquefort just chuckled to himself until I spoke up again.

"So, what's the deal with the frog cage with the chair in it?"

The tiny king/prince was licking honey off of the back of his wrist. "Not that it's any of your business, Troll, but that is the King Mobile. The king must travel in both safety and comfort. So it is written, and so it shall be."

CAGE

JERK-FACE

OGRES

KING MOBILE
(ARTIST RENDERING)

I turned to the two ogres. They were both glaring at the king—clearly not happy about the earlier "disposable" comment. "We carry him in it." Buddy looked away.

BIG BRAVE KING THAT HE IS.

"And you'll carry me in it again, Ogre!!" Roquefort snarled.

With that, Buddy stood up out of the water and walked over to the honey-covered cage. He held it up so we could all get a good look at it. Then, without a word, he turned and—really putting his back into it—launched it into the air. And I don't mean a few feet. That cage and chair sailed into the air like a home run hit.

It came crashing down in the top branches of the flumpfruit tree. Then Buddy quietly walked back to the creek and rejoined the group.

INSUBORDINATION! TREASON!!

The king was losing his mind. "You'll pay for this, you over-grown swamp sponge!!" You could see the panic in his eyes. "How am I, the king, to travel unprotected?? Bad things could befall me!! This is . . . I don't . . ."

The rest of us sat back in the water with our eyes closed and tried our best to tune out the tantrum. I peeked out of the corner of my eye and saw a thin smile slide across Buddy's face. Maybe there was more to the big lug than I had imagined.

· 28 ·

A LITTLE BIT
OF AWKWARD

OUTRAGEOUS!!

Unbelievably, despite our having just pulled his stupid little butt out of the honey, all Roquefort could think about was the injustice of having to hang out with a troll. "A king forced to interact with the lowest . . . the vilest of creatures! A common criminal! An ESCAPEE, no less, and one of the filthy, furry persuasion!"

He'd been going on like this for the last hour. It was getting old, fast, and in my head I was talking

EEEEASY, BLOOD. DOWN, BOY. to my troll blood, trying to keep it calm.

We were all hungry, cranky, sticky and, if I'm being honest, stinky.

"When my father hears about this whole fiasco, he may bring back beheading, I'm just warning you." Roquefort was far from running out of wind.

Seriously?? I mean, we had literally JUST SAVED HIM! I was losing my inner battle.

The little jerk went on. "Or public flogging. Or some kind of new, horrible thing he could do. Maybe something troll-specif—"

WILL YOU SHUT UP, YOU SNIVELING LITTLE TURD??

I was working my ear like crazy, but if I rubbed any harder, I was going to wear the fur off.

"We saved your stupid, ungrateful little butt, so

why don't you PIPE DOWN and let the GROWN-UPS do what we CAME HERE for!" I was all up in the prince's face. I couldn't contain my meltdown. "And your dad LIKES trolls, in case you haven't been paying attention!" I was on fire now. It was like letting a monster out of its cage. "So why don't you just curl up in a ball and WHINE yourself to death. Because I CAN'T TAKE IT ANYMORE."

The king's face turned a royal shade of purple as he turned away and crossed his arms in a huff, quiet at last.

HARRUMPH.

I still had so much anger pouring out of me—it had to go somewhere. I started yelling and jumping up and down and thrashing around while the rest of the group watched, openmouthed. I reached down and started grabbing rocks—big ones—and chucking them as far and hard as my muscles would let me.

This wasn't a coping plan that Gramps had given me, but I hoped it would burn off some energy. Wind up, throw. Wind up, throw. Like an overheated furry pitching machine.

And that was all going well, until . . . my hand slipped.

You may think that with all the fur on a paw, it would be tough for it to get all sweaty and slippery. You would be wrong.

So I went to throw this good-sized rock—probably the size of a healthy Flack Rabbit—when it slipped and that rock went flying out of my paw.

Right. At. Kevin.

Have you ever had one of those moments where you see something happening in slow motion? And there's nothing you can do? This was one of those moments.

I turned just in time to see the rock shoot out sideways and smash Kevin square in the snout. There was a crunch like sitting on a bag of Fritos, and I knew it was going to be bad.

The second I saw blood, I was filled with horrifying shame. He was out cold. His snout was bleeding pretty  badly, and I thought his lip was cut, though it was hard to tell. Chester was there with me, patting Kevin's cheek.

"Kev? I'm so sorry, buddy! Wake up for us, okay?" I was crying again—I felt beyond terrible. Once again I'd let the anger take control—and now my best friend had paid the price.

I was vaguely aware of the prince, laughing it up behind me. He was going on about it to his guards. "Did you see that? That was AWESOME! Hahahaha!"

"I mean seriously. I want that on the royal YouTube page!"

I tuned him out as Kevin's eyelids started fluttering. He let out a groan that made my heart hurt. Then he sat up a bit and spit something out into one of his hooves—a front tooth.

When he saw that and the blood, he passed out again. Just for a moment this time. He sat up and looked at his tooth again.

MY MOM ITH GONNA KILL ME!!

I was relieved that his panic seemed to be overriding the pain.

"That wathn't a baby one! Thath a grown-up one!!"

"I'm so sorry, Kev!" I was blubbering like a Bawling Tree. "I am so, so sorry! I'll get it fixed, I swear. Are you okay??"

It went on like this for a while—me freaking out about hitting him in the face and him freaking out about his tooth. After the anger ran out of me, I felt like an empty husk.

"Zarf, man." Kev kept dabbing at his snout and

lip with a handkerchief. "You buthted my tooth. I mean . . . you've gotta get that anger thtuff under control." He gave me a meaningful look.

THERIOUTHLY.

That sound, the sound of Kev trying to say the word "seriously," got us laughing, even though I felt like doing anything but. I put my head in my paws. "I'm so sorry, guys. You didn't ask for a friend with a nuclear temper."

Chester patted me on the back. "Well. The good news is you're finally starting to throw better than my baby sister."

This got a loud bark of a laugh out of Kevin— and then we were all sitting there giggling like a bunch of idiots.

Kevin was showing me the hole where his tooth had been when our phones started blowing up. First it was Kevin's, then Chester's, and then mine.

Clearly Kevin's and Chester's parents had figured out that they weren't camping at each other's houses. My parents had tried my phone a few times earlier that day, but I'd let it ring.

One by one, we heard the "Bloop" sound indicating that we had voicemails. Everyone was trying to act tough.

Kevin broke first. "I, uh . . . you know. I thould probably check that . . . In cathe it's about a weather pattern or thomething. Not that I want to . . ." He was putting on quite a show.

THERE COULD BE A COLD FRONT MOVING IN OR THOMETHING...

Now it was
Chester's turn.
"Yeah. I should
. . . I should
check mine too.
In case my dad
has, like, a joke-

HE COMES TO ME FOR PUNCH LINES SOMETIMES.

related emergency or something."

Finally, we agreed to play our messages out loud so we could all hear them. I think we were all needing a little taste of home.

Roquefort let out a mean little laugh.

YOU BABIES WANNA SUCK YOUR THUMBS WHILE YOU LISTEN TOO?

We ignored him, and one by one we played our messages from our parents. Kevin's parents were grunting and snorting like they'd lost their minds. Chester's dad was ready to beat someone with his juggling balls. But they all ended their messages saying how much they loved and missed them.

Then I played my parents' messages.

The first was from my mom; the second was my dad; both begging me to stay safe and come straight home. Then there was a message from my gramps. He spoke in a low, sad voice that put a lump in my throat.

"Zarf . . . It's yer gramps . . . . Listen, I feel like this is my fault. Me and all my stupid talk abou' the Belford Way and all tha' crap. So, please, don' pay any attention ta wha' I said, okay? I was jus' a foolish old man flappin' his gums. You jus' come home. . . . This too shall pass, y'know?"

I'd never heard him like this.

"So tha's what I called ta tell ya . . . I love you, boy. Come home safe." There was some fumbling with the phone and then the message ended.

You could have heard a pin drop—until a loud snotty sniffle came from my left. I looked over to find Roquefort in full distress.

The king was suddenly crying up a storm and wiping a big snot strand away with the back of his hand.

"What if my dad got eaten by a stupid giant weasel??" He hitched in a couple of breaths before he began bawling again at full tilt. I froze, unsure of what to do.

Then I slowly reached over, like I was about to pet a snake, and gave the king's back a soft test pat.

When he didn't react, I patted him a few more times before resting my paw on his shoulder.

Suddenly he turned and grabbed on to me, pulling me into some kind of weird, desperate hug. "I MISS HIM SO MU-UH-UH-UCH!"

Kevin, Chester, and the two ogres were all looking at me with shocked expressions. I clearly saw what Chester mouthed to me.

WHAT IN THE...

I eventually brought my arms down and started patting the little jerk on the back again. It seemed to help. I actually felt a little bad for suspecting him of having a part in his dad's disappearance.

"Thanks," I heard him say, in a voice just barely audible.

It's funny how when you see somebody crying that hard, it doesn't matter if they're a total jack-dragon. At that point they're just a person who feels like crud.

29

Enough is
a snuff

After Roquefort got it all out of his system, it was like he suddenly realized where he was. He sat up, put a sneer back on his face, and demanded that we slackers get moving again. Always a charmer, that one.

We had only gone another fifteen minutes when we saw our first glimpses of the Sea of Tomorrow through the trees—something I never thought I'd see. Few had, at least from our village. We all grew quiet, as we knew this meant we were close to the Snuffweasels' lair. Over the salty sea air, my troll sense of smell suddenly picked up a strong smell I can only describe as "snuffy."

"If you knew half as much about comedy as you do about poop, I wouldn't be so concerned about you eventually being my Court Jester." Roquefort enjoyed holding that future boss-employee situation over Chester's head.

"Yeah, well, you're . . ." Chester's face tensed up as he tried to come up with a funny response. "I mean . . . You know. Poop you." He sagged a bit, disappointed in himself.

We gathered in a stand of bushes and quietly waited for night to fall. The young king had a bad case of ants in his pants, and proceeded to fuss and fidget to the point of making us all mental.

CAN YOU SIT STILL??

I HAVE RESTLESS LEG SYNDROME!

GROAN.

When it was good and dark, I broke out John's night-vision goggles.

There was one final hill before the water. I scanned the area, looking for an entrance or any activity.

THE KNOBLE KNIGHT VISION GOGS

Finally, in the green-lit view of the night vision, I saw two Snuffweasels skitter out from behind a large boulder. They startled a squirrel, which took off like a shot. But in two easy bounds, one of the Snuffweasels was on it—and snarfed it down in two gulps like it was a Mutton Taco Supreme.

SNARF
·SNaRf
SNARF

A chill shot up my spine, making my fur stand on end. I thought I'd keep the squirrel-massacre to myself—mostly to keep Kevin from wigging out.

"Okay. I just saw two of them come out of the hill. The entrance must be behind that boulder," I said as Roquefort rudely snatched the goggles out of my hands. "We need a plan."

We started spit-balling ideas that ranged from the impossible to the ridiculous. King Roquefort kept insisting that we needed to make Snuffweasel costumes and infiltrate the lair. He even took out some paper and a quill and drew up a schematic.

Kevin wasn't impressed. "It looks like a big, furry hot dog."

Roquefort rolled his eyes so hard, he almost fell over. "Am I surprised that the pig doesn't appreciate art? I am not."

"Well, it's just a brilliant idea, Your Highness." I handed him back his drawing. "All we need now is a fabric store, a seamstress, a couple of Snuffweasel pelts, and some chicken wire—which of course are all readily available out here in Nowheresville."

The king's face turned red. "Well, I don't hear any brilliant ideas from you losers!" He turned to his ogres. "Anything?? Or are you just going to sit there like a couple of lumps?"

LUMP 1   LUMP 2

"Okay," I started. "We have these guys for some muscle. Maybe we load them up with some of our weapons and send them . . ." I stopped when I heard a twig snap behind me.

Suddenly Snuffweasels were everywhere, bursting through the bushes. Fur and leaves were flying.

I could make out Roquefort's high-pitched squawking, but the rest of our yelling was all blended together.

I saw one of the weasels throw a burlap sack over Kevin and scoop him up, just before another bag came down over me. Everything went dark. I was tossed roughly over a big hairy shoulder, hitting my head on my knee. I could hear my friends' muffled shouts from all around me as I lost consciousness.

* * *

OOF.
OOF.
OOF.

X-RAY
VIEW

When I came to I was bunched up in the bottom of the sack, bouncing against my captor's backside. The smell of the weasels was almost unbearable at this point. You ever smell something so strong, you taste it? It was like that. I was tasting weasel. I started breathing through my mouth and listened for my friends.

Then the sound changed. I assumed we had entered the weasels' lair. There was a growing murmur that scared the wits out of me. It was the sound of a large group of Snuffweasels. My heart plunged into my stomach.

Then, abruptly, all of the snarling, grunting, and snuffling stopped. So did my Snuffweasel. Everything became still, except my heart, which

CANNONBALL!

was pounding so hard, it was making my teeth shimmy.

There was complete silence, and then quietly, from somewhere off to my right, I heard Kevin muttering to himself. "Ohhh no. Oh no. Got the panic thweatth. I'm hyperventilating . . . Need a paper bag to breathe into. Wait . . . I'm IN a bag. How can I be hyperventilating inthide a bag? Oh dear oh dear oh dear . . ."

He was cut off by what sounded like a loud bark that echoed off the walls of the lair. Then I was up-ended and dumped onto the cold, wet floor—right on my head.

I sat up and saw the others being dumped from their sacks as well. We were in the middle of an enormous cavern. There were those rock things hanging from the ceiling—I can never remember if they're stalactites or stalagmites. But most alarm-ingly, we were surrounded by maybe twenty-five hideous, drooling Snuffweasels.

DROOL→

I saw one weasel scurry over to the wall. There was a small hole there with a crude arrow painted above it. The weasel barked some kind of command into the wall, and it came out amplified by about five hundred percent.

BAARK!

It was so loud, it shook the rock walls. And then more weasels were pouring into the room, as if called to duty. Faster than I could have imagined, they had us all bound securely in rope and scooped us up again. The other weasels cleared a path as we were carried forward.

BWAAAA!! I'M TOO RICH AND HANDSOME TO DIE!

My nose picked up something that smelled like one of the marinades my mom uses when she cooks. I was thinking that was kind of odd when the Snuff-weasels stepped back to reveal a huge vat full of oily brown liquid. And there, tied up right in the middle of it, the liquid right up to his chest, was our king. The real king. King Cheznott. The king's eyes went wide with surprise when he saw us. "Oh, dear."

30

IN THE
THICK OF IT

The brown goop in the vat was colder than I'd expected. One taste told me that it was, indeed, a marinade. Maybe a light balsamic vinaigrette. Floating around us in the liquid were several whole onions and peppers, as well as nine or ten large, whole fish. Clearly they were looking to spice us up before dinnertime. Great. Just great.

Roquefort, Chester, Kevin, and the ogres were tossed into the sauce as well. The prince ('cause he was a prince again, right? I mean, we found the king) came up sputtering and gasping for air. He began slopping his way through the sauce toward his dad. "Father! I've . . . I've come to save you . . . from these horrid beasts!"

It was tough going, hopping through the liquid, and he was getting winded.

"Thank you, my son. Thank you." They couldn't really hug, so the king and prince just sort of leaned against each other awkwardly for a couple of seconds.

I fought my way through the goop to the king as well. "Your Highness. We came to help, but I fear we've fallen victims ourselves. I'm terribly sorry."

The king turned away as I saw his eyes well up. He stayed that way for a minute, sniffing loudly.

"I don't cry for myself, furry one." He turned back around. "I had come to terms with being eaten.

Oh, but that it were only me. I fear the four men I arrived with were already made into a large Kingsmen Pot Pie. A horrible business."

That made me shudder.

"Listen. King Cheznott. If we're going to die here, I want to thank you. On behalf of my family. Since I can remember, my parents have gushed about you and all you've done for trollkind." I heard the prince make a disgusted noise behind me.

A sad smile crawled across the king's face.

"Well, I appreciate that. If we get out of this mess, I give you my word I'll do more. Trolls are good people in my book."

We stood there nodding our heads for a minute or so.

I looked over at Kevin, who was wide-eyed and shivering.

"Hey Kev. You okay?" I sidled over and nudged him.

Chester had waded over as well. "I could tell a few jokes. Maybe lighten the mood a bit?"

Kevin looked at him sideways. "I thintherely with you wouldn't."

Chester was undeterred. "C'mon."

Kevin snapped. "Cut it out, Chethter! Not now. Ethpethially right now! I'd rather not go to my death with one of your thtupid jokths rattling around in my head!" I'd never seen Kevin like this.

Chester looked a bit hurt. "Fine. But don't come crawling to me for the punch line later."

At that point, my troll nose picked up the smell of smoke. I spun around and saw, on the other side of the room, a group of Snuffweasels lighting a fire under a huge cast-iron cauldron.

Oh, that wasn't good. Not good at all.

I took a good look around, and what I saw was pretty alarming. Scattered around the room were tables carved out of rock. One table held what looked like a meat grinder and a long string of sausage links—which made me gulp audibly.

I was trying not to think about what that sausage was made from when I got a face full of balsamic juice.

SPLORT

I looked over, disbelieving, to find the prince
giving me his best innocent look.

He had a little trickle of marinade below his lip.
Apparently his dad had looked away and he'd spit
it at me.

"SERIOUSLY?" I shouted at him. "NOW??
You're even an immature little snot NOW??"

He looked at his dad. "I have no idea what this
troll is yammering about." Then he turned back
and gave me one of his greasiest smiles.

I swiped out with my leg and
knocked the prince's feet out from
under him. And under he went.

The king looked up at me,
surprised. I looked back, expect-
ing to get royally (literally!) chewed out. But then a
small smile flashed across his face—so fast, I almost
missed it. "He deserved that. Now help him up."

I reached out with my leg again, this time to give the prince something to hold on to. He righted himself and once again came up sputtering and gasping for air.

GASP!
SPUTTER.

"TROLL!" he shouted once he'd found his footing. "You will regret this day, you filthy, hairy—" He abruptly stopped.

I followed his line of vision. Standing behind me at the edge of the vat were two of the larger Snuffweasels.

KISS THE COOK

They were clearly deciding which one of us to cook first. Their eyes lingered on Kevin for a bit—who started drooling and frothing at the mouth and rolling his eyes around in his head.

"What are you doing??" I whispered, confused.

"Hopefully I'm making them think I have Mad Pig ditheathe."

WHOOoo! CRATHY PiG MEAT HeRe. NoT GooD EATiNG!

As those weasels kept pointing at Kevin and licking their chops, my blood started to boil. I felt my ears go hot, and I heard that familiar low growl start up in my throat.

GRRRRRRRRRRRR

But I also remembered my gramps's advice about channeling my anger. I needed to do things right this time. So I let it simmer, as best I could—just in case it could help at the right moment. It felt like having a secret weapon in my pocket.

The two cooks suddenly changed their minds. One pointed at the king and before we knew what was happening, they had netted the king and were pulling him out of the vat.

Roquefort, understandably, freaked out. "NN-NOOO!!! Not my dad!!"

TAKE THE TROLL! TAKE THE TROLLLL!!

But the Snuffweasels had flopped the good and honorable king down on a table covered in flour and bread crumbs and were beginning to roll him back and forth. I realized with a jolt that they were breading him like a pork chop.

WELL HONESTLY. I NEVER!

The king was bravely calling out to his son, yelling through the occasional mouth full of breading. "You can do it, son! If you get out . . . out of here, you can rule Notswin in my stead!" He sneezed as one of the weasels ground some pepper over him. "You can be a good and kind king!"

Yeah. Right.

The indignity of that pepper and the unbearable idea of Roquefort being king again were the final straw. And that, friends, is when I let my inner Furry Fury out of his cage. In my head I pictured a funnel, pushing all of that power into the exact place I needed it. I bore down, thinking about all of my Belford ancestors before me—and with all of my troll rage and all of my troll strength, I pushed against the ropes around me.

When the ropes broke, it was with a noise like a shot. They went flying. The rest of the weasels turned at the sound, and came toward the vat. I started untying Kevin, since I thought he might be next on the breading table—but the knot was so tight, I was just going to have to pull it apart with good old TrollPower©.

"Kevin, I need to break the others' ropes! As soon as you're loose, go straight for the chef. You need to attack!"

Kevin was dumbfounded. "WHAAAT?"

HAVE YOU MET ME?

"There's something I haven't told you, Kevin." I could see the rope starting to give way where I was pulling at it. "Snuffweasels taste just like mutton. It's a little-known fact. So I need you to channel every ounce of your love for mutton, and go gnaw on some of that sweet, sweet Snuffweasel meat."

He stared back for just a moment as his ropes

snapped and fell away. I think he realized I was completely full of it, but he suddenly got a steely look in his eye, took a deep breath, and leaped out of the liquid.

FOR MY LOVE OF THE KING AND/OR MUTTON!!

Several Snuffweasels grabbed at him, but he slipped through their paws like . . . like a greased pig. The weasel in the apron was now carrying the king across the cave to the cauldron. In three bounds, Kevin was on him, clamping down on his furry shin with a loud crunch. The cook dropped the king and howled like . . . well, he howled like there was a pig chewing on his leg.

AAAIIGGHH!!

I quickly popped the ropes on Chester, the prince, and the two ogres. Buddy and the other one wasted no time in tackling three weasels between the two of them.

I turned, and like the well-trained fish-slapper I am, started slapping dead fish out of the vat—right at the approaching weasels. I never realized how good my aim was, but I was hitting bull's-eyes every time. The fish were slamming into the weasels' faces and those that didn't just go sprawling were left staggering around wiping the stinging goo out of their eyes. I slapped fish until there were only vegetables left. Then I slapped vegetables.

My projectiles ran out, and I was jumping out of the vat when Chester yelled after me. "What do I do? We don't have our weapons!"

I landed with a splat.

JUST DO SOMETHING! ANYTHING!

He reached down into the back of his pants and pulled out—I kid you not—that stupid rubber chicken he always carried around. He started swinging it around over his head and ran off into the action.

I ran to a table and grabbed a string of several large, heavy sausages. I swung them around a few times—perfect nunchuck substitutes.

MEAT CHUCKS

I spun around and clubbed the nearest weasel on the ear. That was when I heard Chester yell at the top of his lungs.

KNOCK, KNOCK!!

I turned around to glare at him. "Seriously? That's what you came up with?"

Chester, standing there with the rubber chicken hanging from his hand, spoke quietly out of the corner of his mouth, as if the Snuffweasels could understand us. "I'm 'Using My Strengths,' nimrod," he whispered, making air quotes with his fingers.

But I wasn't the only one who had stopped what he was doing. Every Snuffweasel in the room had come to an abrupt halt. It was like in an old film when someone scratches the needle off of a record. They were all staring at Chester, except the chef, who was still struggling to get Kevin's teeth out of his shin meat.

31

KNOCK, KNOCK

"**N**ok-Nok?" one of the weasels said quietly, looking to one of its buddies.

Chester looked uncomfortable under the gaze of the entire room, but he said it again. "Knock . . . knock?"

The weasels all started looking around nervously at each other, their eyes getting wider. "Nok-Nok?"

Now I'd seen everything. Were they afraid of knock-knock jokes? Or had Chester's reputation for unfunniness even made its way to the weasel world? Whatever it was, it had sketched them out pretty badly.

"Knock, knock," I yelled, and one of the weasels turned to me with its paws out, as if to say "Easy, buddy."

"Start yelling it!" I cried to the others. "They don't like it."

And so, sounding like a bunch of idiots, Chester, Kevin, the ogres, the king, and I all started yelling at the top of our lungs, "Knock, knock! Knock, knock!" I ran over to that hole in the wall with the arrow and yelled into it as loud as I could. It made the ground shake, and a few of those stalactite/stalagmite things came crashing down.

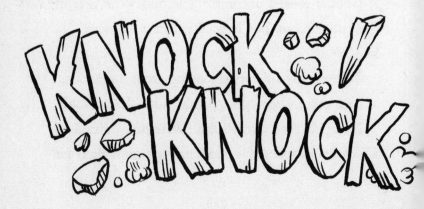

Complete chaos took over. It was as if our words were stinging the weasels' ears. They ran around like they were in a Three Stooges movie, babbling and slamming into each other. Then they started racing out of the hole in the back of the cave.

One brave one took a final swipe at me as he passed and I meat-chucked it across the back of the head. It fell in a crumpled heap.

KNOCK, KNOCK, FURBAG.

And then . . . just like that, they were gone.

"Everybody okay?" I asked, panting, my hair all fuzzed out like a Chia pet.

"NO!" Kevin was starting to shake. "NO, I'M PRETTY MUCH THE OPPOTHITE OF OKAY!!" Chester had his hands on his knees, his head down. The king, shaken, was making his way over to us on wobbly legs, wiping breading out of his eyes.

"We did it," I said quietly. It wasn't a yell of victory. We were too tired for that. Too out of breath. But Buddy the ogre looked up from where he sat on the ground and gave me a tired high five.

SMACK

There was some more panting and gasping for air before the king quietly spoke up.

"Where's my son?"

I spun around to find the prince, but he was gone. The only sign of him was a trail of tiny sauce footprints that led out of the cave. He'd fled. Typical.

* * *

The prince's footsteps led out of the same opening
through which the Snuffweasels had fled. We all ran
that way and found ourselves moving down a rocky
corridor. About halfway down, we stumbled over
a pile of our weapons and backpacks. We grabbed
our weapons of choice and moved on at a run. I was
in the lead when I saw sun-lit
sand and heard the
crashing of
waves.

At the opening of the cave, I froze. The others
plowed into the back of me, but I didn't budge. It
took my (admittedly slow) brain a moment to register what I was looking at.

We had come out into a small inlet. High walls of
rock surrounded the beach. The sun was just clearing the horizon.

There in the sand, maybe ten feet in front of me,

was the prince. He was sitting on the ground, leaning back and frozen in place. Maybe ten feet beyond him was the largest Lava Dragon I had ever laid eyes on. I swear to you it was the length of a football field from head to tail. A fire-breathing 747 with feet.

A small trickle of fire and smoke would occasionally drift up from its nostril. Scattered around its feet were a number of Snuffweasel bodies. Some were bent in unnatural ways. Others looked singed, and if you think burnt hair smells bad, burnt Snuffweasel hair is a new, epic kind of disgusting. I heard Kevin behind me.

"Oh, I really can't take much more of thith. No, thir."

I HAVE A NERVOUTH THTOMACH, YOU KNOW.

The prince let out a tiny whimper and spoke quietly out of the corner of his mouth. "I think this is Knock-Knock. I'd like to thank you morons ever so much for calling out to him over and over again."

"What?" I asked. "How would that even—"

At that moment, the dragon opened its mouth like a huge, fanged garage door, and let out two insanely loud roars. They shook the rock walls around us, and sounded for all the world like "GNAAAAWK GNAAAAWK!!!"

I heard Chester behind me, talking under his breath so quietly, I could barely hear him. "Okay . . . That sure as heck sounded like 'Knock-Knock.'"

THIS FREAKIN' LIZARD'S STEALING MY ACT.

The dragon let go with two even louder roars that really did sound an awful lot like the beginning of a knock-knock joke. We all felt a blast of heat and smelled what had to be roasted Snuffweasel on its breath. My mouth fell open and I felt my sword drop out of my numb fingers. The prince spoke again, quietly.

I MAY NEED A FRESH PAIR OF LEGGINGS.

So this was what the Snuffweasels had been freaking out about. I heard nervous chittering and realized they were cowering behind boulders all around us.

NOK-NOK?

I was bending down to pick up my sword when a shadow fell over us. The tail of the giant dragon swung around like a whip. It violently slammed into everyone but me, grazing the top of my hair.

Everyone was hit, but Kevin and Chester took the brunt of it. They both flew about ten feet before smashing into the walls of the cove—where they crumpled to the ground like rag dolls. Seeing my friends broken and discarded like that was like a knife to my heart—and what pumped out was a hot kind of troll blood like I had never felt. I jumped back into the opening of the cave to dodge the tail as it came back around. I was beyond furious. I was a hurricane of hate aimed straight at that dragon . . . and when it came back the next time, I was going to be ready.

HURRICANE
ZARF
CATEGORY
10

I assumed the fight stance the Knoble Knight had taught me. I held the sword in the Western grip he'd shown me. I felt the blood pumping through my veins, giving me strength, and it felt good. It felt RIGHT.

The tail smashed into the cave entrance, rocks exploding everywhere. I jumped forward with all my strength and all of my anger and planted my sword to the hilt. Holding on took every bit of Troll-Power © I could muster, but there was no way I was letting go. I was pulled free of the cave and lifted into the sky as I hiked a leg over the tail and held on for dear life. The ground rushed away from me.

The dragon was roaring so loud it shook the air around me like it was made of Jell-O. Old Knock-Knock's attention was no longer on the prince, that was for sure. I saw the royal squirt on the beach below me, hightailing it for cover behind a pile of driftwood.

The dragon was spinning in circles and snapping at me like a dog chasing its tail. It almost got me on one pass. One of its dagger-sized teeth grazed my leg and opened a six-inch gash.

Holding on with my legs, I yanked out the sword and started chopping at that tail like some lunatic beaver trying to take down a tree. A big, scaly, lava-spewing tree. I put everything I had into the hacking, and let out a yell of pure rage. I'm not sure what I yelled, and I may have sounded like a psychotic marshdevil—but I didn't care.

DIE, YOU OVERSIZED AMPHIBIAN!!

Now, keep in mind that I was half out of my gourd with anger, okay . . . but have you ever seen a cartoon where a person cuts off the limb of a tree, and they cut off the part they happen to be sitting on? And they fall? Yeah. I did that with the tail. Like I've said, trolls aren't rocket scientists.

I rode the severed end of the tail like a bucking bronco as it fell to the beach. And when I hit the ground, I hit hard. Really hard. Like, I-couldn't-move hard.

I was lying there trying to catch my breath when I suddenly had a furious skyscraper of a Lava Dragon in my face. I couldn't sit up. Couldn't even slither backward.

A huge glob of lava drool fell from one of the monster's lips and landed an inch from my head. It sizzled into the sand, throwing off heat like a furnace.

Then, and I swear on a stack of Knoble Knight comics this is true, the dragon spoke. It spoke!

To give you some idea of how startling this was— a talking dragon—imagine how you'd feel if your refrigerator started dancing around the kitchen singing "Happy Birthday." That's how stunned I was when this monster piped up.

AND MANY MOOOOORE!

"TROLLLLLLL." How can I explain that voice? It was so deep, it sounded like a cross between Darth Vader's voice and someone farting through a tuba. The vibrations shook my innards like Jell-O, and I suddenly felt light-headed. "PATHETIC, LOWLY TROLL. YOU THINK YOU CAN BEST MEEE?"

I mustered up every ounce of bravery and anger left in me. "I'm not sure. But I'm willing to die trying."

"OH," it boomed in response, "THAT CAN BE ARRANGED."

The dragon opened its mouth insanely wide. I'd seen a show on Dragon Week on the Animal Channel and knew this wasn't a good thing. I was about to get incinerated in a gusher of lava. I could see the nasty-looking lava tube in the back of the dragon's mouth start to jiggle and quiver as the hot liquid made its way up from the creature's insides.

← SO NASTY

It started to make a hissing noise like those steamer things at Starbucks. I closed my eyes and hoped it would be over quickly.

Then I heard a blast of trumpets. My first thought was, "Okay. This must be what happens when you die." A nice little musical send-off as you head off to the great hereafter.

HOW ABOUT SOME EARTH, WIND & FIRE AS YOU GO?

But Knock-Knock heard it too. Its mouth snapped shut and that enormous, awful head snapped around to find the source of the sound.

WHAT IN THE...

We both looked up to the top of the rock wall surrounding us in time to see a horse's head poke up into view.

The rest of the horse followed, and there was something humped over the horse's back. It took me a moment to make out what it was.

32

911

The lump on the horse did its best to sit up, and I realized it was John . . . the Knoble Knight himself. I have never been so happy to see someone in all of my life.

John, still weak and barely able to hold himself up, raised one hand. He held it there and shouted, "APPROACH!"

At that point, maybe fifty members of the king's army stepped up and into view. Every one of them was armed with bow and arrow—pointed at my good buddy Knock-Knock.

John dropped his arm and shouted, "FIRE!" There was a collective twang, and the sky filled with arrows, sounding like a swarm of bees. The dragon tried to scramble backward, shouting "NO NO NO NO NOOO!" but most of the arrows found their mark.

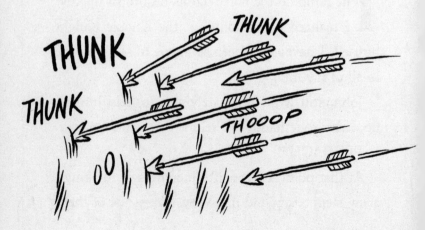

I would imagine that to a beast of that size the arrows felt like a bunch of bee stings. But having been stung by a single bee one summer at Damptowel Beach, I can't blame the dragon for what followed.

First, I tell you . . . this is the truth. The dragon yelled what sounded like, "YEEOOWWCHHAA!"

That sounds ridiculous, but I swear that's what it said. Then it scrambled backward, swatting at its side with its enormous wings and roaring.

"OH, THAT SMARTS! OH, FOR THE LOVE OF ALL THINGS SCALY, THAT HURTS LIKE THE DICKENS!!"

The beach shook, and sand flew up from the wind it was creating. Then the giant beast got all tangled up in its wounded tail and flopped over backward into the surf. There was a squeal coming from it that reminded me of the time Kevin stepped on a pudding snake behind the school.

"SALT WATER IN THE WOUND!!" it roared on. "NOT COOL! NOT COOL AT ALL!!"

EEEEE!!

I heard John yelling at his men to reload. And then Kevin and Chester were staggering up beside me. Kevin was stumbling around picking up rocks and chucking them at Knock-Knock—not very effectively, but I appreciated the effort. Chester had grabbed my sword from wherever it had fallen, and was swinging it above his head. Then, with precision timing, he brought the sword down and lopped off a dragon toe the size of a golden retriever. The toe flipped and flopped around a bit on its own, which made Kevin scream and me feel all squirmy inside.

AND THIS LITTLE PIGGIE GOT NONE.

The dragon screamed bloody murder and grabbed at its foot. "MY PINKIEEEE!" It flopped around a few more times and started flapping its wings. In a few swooshing beats, it lifted awkwardly off of the ground. It hovered long enough to shoot the three of us a look of pure hatred that curdled my blood. "STUPID, LOUSY, NO GOOD, MEDDLING . . . **STINK DRAGONS!!**"

The dragon whipped out its injured foot, clocking me across the forehead so hard, I saw stars and collapsed back on the sand. Then it flew off in a hurry, another volley of arrows from the men flying after it.

I looked up to the top of the rock wall and my eyes met John's. He winked and gave me a thumbs-up. Another horse stepped up beside him and as my vision dimmed, I saw my favorite lunch lady riding high on its back.

When I woke up, I had a headache like someone was sticking snagglethorns into my eyes. Goldie was leaning over me and wiping my face with a damp cloth.

Kevin was jumping around, acting out our fight with the Snuffweasels to the amusement of several of the king's men.

AND I JUTHT BIT HITH LEG CLEAN OFF! ONE CHOMP!

Chester was sitting in the sand beside me, his head bandaged. He had a goofy sideways grin on his face. "Hey, Zarf. I just thought of the perfect knock-knock joke. Wanna hear it?"

The look I gave him must have said a lot, because his smile faded a bit and he looked away, patting my leg. "Never mind, buddy. I mean, have you seen the power of my knock-knock jokes? But . . . never you mind."

I looked across the sand to where John was still lying on the back of his horse. When he saw me looking his way, a big cheesy grin spread across his face. He gave me another thumbs-up and mouthed the words: "You did good, kid."

Then it was lights out again.

· 33 ·

BACK-TO-SCHOOL SPECIAL

On our first day back to school, Kevin came by my house at the usual time, and my mom sent us off with enough mutton to feed the Royal Army. We were both sporting some nasty cuts and bruises, but Kev's tooth had been glued back in the day before. I had a pretty good shiner, and Kevin was sporting a couple of fashionable Sponge Bob Band-Aids.

We met Chester by the football field. He didn't look any better than we did.

As we walked in the front door of good old Cotswin, I wasn't sure what to expect. Pats on the back? Applause?

It was a completely new feeling for me, but I was pretty sure my star was about to rise. I was feeling pretty stinkin' good about how this day would go.

We stepped in the front door, and I was assaulted by a horrible smell, like the sewer had backed up and they'd stopped collection of the after-lunch garbage. This place had seriously gone downhill in my absence! But I was quickly distracted when Sten Vinders, one of the more popular goats in the class above us, approached me.

"I heard about your big adventure! You have a minute to talk?"

I gave him a big grin. "Sure!" (Anything for my adoring fans, you know.) Kevin and Chester said they'd see me later and headed off to their classes.

"So, tell me all about it!" Sten seemed really eager to talk to me. This was crazy! I was a flippin' rock star!

So I started in on the tale, as Sten and several others followed me down the hall to my locker.

"Well, I don't know if you've ever seen a Snuff-weasel up close, but they're quite a bit larger than you might think."

Sten seemed really fascinated. "Yeah?? Tell me more!"

So, I went on. There was a group of people walking with me now, and they were all really into it. I noticed that smell again as we moved down the hall. It was impossible to miss! Had the whole school gotten used to it? Gross! But I kept going with my tale.

AND DON'T GET ME STARTED ON HONEY BOGS! NOT JUST ANYONE CAN LOOK DEATH IN THE EYE LIKE...

As I stepped up to my locker, the smell threatened to overwhelm me. I was starting to think somebody had let off a stink bomb in the boys' bathroom—or Mr. Hirsch had been in there again. But as I worked my combination lock, still yammering on,

I realized that the smell was coming from my locker. I popped it open.

The wave of blinding stink hit me first, making me close my eyes and pull back like I'd been Tasered. Then the laughter started.

There, on the top shelf of my locker, was a small Stink Dragon, calmly licking its nether parts. A real Stink Dragon. An awful, smelly, gooey, nasty green little Stink Dragon.

Its horrible-smelling dragon goop was oozing all over my books, and hanging in long snot-like strands from the shelf.

It seemed like half the school had gathered around me laughing—no one laughing harder than good old Sten. Stupid goat-lookin' son of a no good . . .

Somebody behind me yelled out, "Looks like you got yerself a little mascot!"

The only reason I didn't have a troll explosion is that I was more embarrassed than angry. Just then the tiny Stink Dragon decided to bolt for freedom, leaping out of the locker and directly into my face.

SPLORT

GAAA!!

I flailed around to get it off of me and lost my balance. I went down on my back with a thud—much to Sten's delight.

The dragon skittered off down the hall as I lay there on my back, gagging and trying to wipe the foul stink-goop out of my eyes.

That's when Sten stepped up and squatted down in front of me, chuckling.

The rest of the day didn't go much better. Sure, I really did get a couple of pats on the back—including one from Principal Haggard, who pulled me aside and told me how glad he was to have me back. But mostly, it was business as usual.

I wasn't sure if people didn't know yet what we had done, or if they did, and just couldn't bring themselves to feel good for a troll. I suspected it was the troll thing.

That afternoon after school, there was a ceremony scheduled in the school gym. Official notices had gone up all around the kingdom inviting anyone who could come and they came in droves. Practically the entire village was there, crammed into the creaky old bleachers. Tree gnomes lined the rafters.

BEST SEAT IN THE HOUSE, LOSERS!

Trumpets blasted at three o'clock and the whole room fell silent except for one elf in the back who yelled out "Baba Booey!" and was shushed.

We were sitting on a riser in the middle of the gym facing the crowd.

There was more fanfare as the king—the real

king—stepped out from behind a heavy velvet curtain and hopped up onto the riser. He smiled over at all of us lined up in folding chairs, and then walked straight up to the Knoble Knight. John leaned forward so the king could speak into his ear.

The king took John's hands in his own and smiled as they shared a brief exchange. I was close, but I couldn't make out what was said. Their brief conversation ended with genuine laughter from both, and the king wiping away a tear.

Then King Cheznott crossed the riser and stepped up on a step stool behind the podium.

CITIZENS OF NOTSWIN!

"I have come here today to bestow thanks."

Then he prattled on for a while about this and that. About his responsibilities as the king, and about the bravery of the men who were still lost. That part was sad, but man, could this king talk.

I was idly looking over the faces in the crowd, when I spotted Sierra. (Yes, the super-cute one. Let it go!) She was looking away, but suddenly she looked over and our eyes met. She smiled and gave me a quick double thumbs-up. It was exactly as cute as you'd expect, and though it made me feel warm all over, let's move on. I'm not writing a romance novel here.

The king went on and on long enough that Chester drew a cartoon of it.

YAK YAK
BLAH BLAH
BLAH

So when he finally got to the thanking us part, we all perked up.

"These boys here . . . with some help from this lovely lunch woman and brave knight . . . saved my life. And I thank them. Deeply. There will of course be a reward to split between you."

I saw my family in the front row. My mom was pride-crying her way through a box of tissues, but my dad and Gramps just kept giving me thumbs-ups and winking at me.

SNIFF

"But there was one young man who showed exceptional bravery, astounding courage . . . and a never-give-up attitude we could all learn from. That young man . . ."

Kevin reached over and patted me on the leg as the king paused for dramatic effect.

"That young man is my son, Prince Roquefort P. Cheznott. Roquefort? Could you come say a few words?"

The crowd cheered as Roquefort emerged from behind the curtain and crossed the stage triumphantly.

Kevin let out an indignant little grunt and Chester said a quiet "What the . . . ?"

"My people!" the prince began. "Thank you for the much-deserved applause, but please . . . take your seats."

He let the crowd settle down a bit before going on. Just that fast, I was starting to feel queasy.

"Am I a hero?" the little runt began.

PROBABLY.

Chester groaned.

"But I mean, am I the greatest hero Notswin has ever seen? Maybe I am . . . Maybe I am . . ."

As His Wonderfulness went on, I leaned over to Kevin and whispered in his ear.

I NEED SOME AIR OR I'M GONNA HURL.

Kevin leaned out and looked at Chester. "Our friend here could use some air."

Chester looked blankly at us both for a moment before speaking in a low voice. "Now that you mention it, a little fresh air sounds like just the ticket."

And with that, the three of us stood up and walked off of the makeshift stage. There was an audible gasp from the crowd. The prince noticed.

"Am I the single greatest . . . greatest . . ."

But we just headed for the gymnasium doors as the crowd murmured and scooched out of our way.

WHERE DO YOU THINK YOU'RE GOING?

"Get back here NOW, you peasants! Your prince is speaking!!" I didn't look, but I could tell from his voice that the royal blood was really pumping now. We kept going.

Standing at attention in front of the exit door was none other than Buddy the ogre. I stepped up and he stared at me, blocking our way.

We stood there looking at each other for a moment before a hint of a smile crossed his face and he stepped aside. He pushed the lever, swung the door open, and held up a fist—which I bumped.

Roquefort went on. "STINK DRAGONS! That's all you are and all you'll ever be!!"

I'll admit, right then when he called us that most awful of insults, I felt a surge of troll blood. My face flushed for just a second before I took a deep breath and silently told my anger to chill out.

The prince was going nuts as we walked out the door. He was really ramping up as the door slowly closed behind us. "If I stepped on you all, I wouldn't bother to reach down and scrape you off the bottom of my royal . . ."

And then we couldn't hear him anymore, and it was wonderful.

I stretched and took a deep breath, smelling the sweet odor of grundlethrush on the breeze.

Kevin smiled. "Absolutely. But do you care if we swing by the butcher shop first? I need to see a girl about some meat."

We laughed, and set off for a day just absolutely packed full of whatever felt right.

THE END

Follow Zarf and his friends
on their next adventure in

LiFE OF ZARF
THE TROLL WHO CRIED WOLF

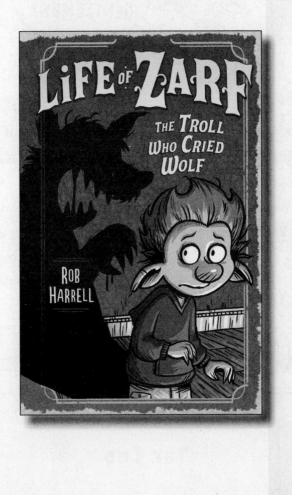